# Smoke in Love

## FOUR20 BAE

# ELLE WRIGHT

**Smoke in Love**

Excerpt from *It's Not Me, It's You*
copyright @ 2021 by Elle Wright

Excerpt from *Some Kind of Love*
copyright @ 2023 by Elle Wright

Elle Wrights Books, LLC
Ypsilanti, Michigan
www.ElleWright.com

**Copy Editor/Proofreading:**
Melissa Ringsted
There For You Editing

Cover Design:
Sherelle Green

# Smoke in Love

**Alaiya**

In the wake of my shattered marriage, I found myself at a crossroads, finally free to pursue my own desires. Filing for divorce was my chance to break loose and do what I want to do. You know what they say about best laid plans... I didn't plan on *him*, though.

I tried to refrain myself, but he's weakening my resistance. Especially when he shows up at my door with desire in his eyes and one of the items from my celebratory divorce list in his hand.

**Spencer**

It should've been business as usual. After all, we've worked together for years. Yet, Alaiya is much too tempting. She has a plan, a bucket list of sorts. So do I. My plan is to give her what she needs—and everything she never knew she wanted.

The game is set, and my goal is clear. Getting her to fall will require challenging every expectation. Convincing her to risk everything will mean breaking every rule. Yet, persuading her to take a chance at a love that defies all odds will be essential in winning her forever.

*Four20 Bae... When couples burn together from one end to the other. Make sure you check out all the stories in this multi-author series.*

Dear Reader

When I tell you that life has been life-ing!!! Yes, it has.

The idea for Smoke in Love came from my desire to match someone from the ever-growing Young family with the Cross family. These two families have been swirling around each other's orbits for quite some time and I knew it was time for two of them to get busy. LOL

And let me tell you something … Spencer and Alaiya were a breath of fresh air!

Two 40+ characters (Grown & Sexy for the win). *Check*.

A lot of life lived between them. *Check*.

An undeniable chemistry. *Check*.

Vibes. *Check*.

BOOM! Destiny fulfilled.

I loved writing their romance! There's something about a friends-to-lovers story that gives me all the feels. These two characters had a history, a quiet understanding of each other that I found endearing.

I hope you enjoy the ride to their HEA!

Love,

Elle

www.ellewright.com

## Recommended Reading

*Smoke in Love* is a crossover novel pairing up the Young Family and the Cross family.

You first met the mysterious Ryker Cross in my novel, IT'S NOT ME, IT'S YOU. Then, Maddox Cross found his *Happily Ever After* with Sloane Wilson in my novella, TEN CHRISTMAS SHOTS.

Then, I kicked off the Smoke and Burn series with a prelude, SOME KIND OF LOVE, featuring Taylor Cross and Keon Webb.

If you'd like to get acquainted with this family before you read, I recommend starting with that story.

———

*About those Youngs...*

IT'S NOT ME, IT'S YOU is book one in the Young In Love Series, followed by IT'S NOT LOVE, IT'S BUSINESS, then IT'S NOT THE HOOKUP, IT'S THE CHASE, IT'S NOT THEM, IT'S ONLY HER, and IT'S NOT FOREVER, IT'S FOR NOW.

The Young Family have appeared in several of my other novels/novellas.

Paityn Young found everlasting love in my novella, HER LITTLE SECRET. The twins, Blake and Bliss made their first appearance in her story.

Blake Young appeared again as Ryleigh's friend in my Once Upon a Baby novella, BEYOND EVER AFTER.

Duke Young burst onto the scene in my Pure Talent novels, THE WAY YOU TEMPT ME and THE WAY YOU HOLD ME. And he stole the show.

Dallas Young made her presence known in my Once Upon a Funeral novella, FINDING COOPER.

Then… The Young in Love Series kicked off with Blake's story, IT'S NOT ME, IT'S YOU. Next, Dallas found her happily every after in IT'S NOT LOVE, IT's BUSINESS. And, Dexter hooked Charley in IT'S NOT THE HOOKUP, IT'S THE CHASE.

Meet their extended family in TEN CHRISTMAS SHOTS, which is a follow-up of my first historical romance set in the 1980s, MADE TO HOLD YOU.

Please Note: Several of these stories take place around the same time. Some events may happen in multiple books from a different POV.

www.ellewright.com

# Content Notes

Hi again,

I love to be surprised when I read a book. But I fully recognize that every reader is not like me. If you haven't read an Elle Wright book before, I feel like I should let you know a few things before you dive in.

*SMOKE IN LOVE* contains sexual content, profanity, and sensitive subjects that some may find triggering.

Trigger Warnings include but are not limited to:

Death of a family member (mentioned)
Addiction (mentioned)
Parental Neglect
Drug use (This is a Four20 Anthology, after all)

*For all those who loved, lost, then found love again*

# *Playlist*

Listen on Spotify or Apple Music!

*His Prologue*

**Spencer**

*Twenty-Five Years Ago*

The eerie silence should've been my first clue that something was up, but I entered the crowded house anyway. Scanning the room, I made eye contact with every muthafucka there. The threat was unspoken, they knew what was up. I never had to say a word.

"Where is she?" I grumbled.

My homeboy, O, pointed to the hallway leading to the bedrooms. "Man, I didn't give it to her."

My jaw clenched, and I fought the urge to fuck that nigga up. Slowly, I blew out a breath. "Who did?"

Oscar didn't say anything, but I followed his gaze to the culprit. Without another word, I stomped over to that punk-ass fool, Fred, and hemmed him up against the wall. "Tell me why I shouldn't break every damn bone in your body right now."

"I'm not— Man, stop. I didn't d-do anything," Fred stammered, "she's a grown-ass woman. How was I supposed to know?"

Gripping his shirt harder, I pulled back, then slammed him against the wall. "I made it clear a long time ago that if you fuck with Laiya, I will fuck you up."

"She's not hurt." Fred's sister, Shaunie, stood at the door of the kitchen, a bottle of water in hand. "I made her lay down. But he's right. What we look like tellin' a groan-ass woman she can't do what the hell she wants to do?"

Even with her assurances, even though she made a valid point, the rage building inside of me hadn't waned. "Shaunie, I don't want to hear that shit. Someone called me and told me she was in trouble. When I got here, muthafuckas lookin' at me like somebody did something to her. How you think I'm supposed to react?"

"Calm yo' ass down, then," she said, walking over to me. "I told you … she's fine." She motioned to my fists. "You gon' let him go now?"

Reluctantly, I released him. Turning to the fellas in the room, I gestured to the door. "All y'all can get the fuck out."

Shaunie planted a hand on her hips. "Nigga, this is *my* house."

"You must've misunderstood me," I told her. "You might pay the rent here, but I own this shit."

"What the fuck?" she exclaimed, flailing her hands in the air.

But I was already on my way to the bedroom. "Now," I clarified.

"For *her*?" Shaunie shouted.

I stilled, that question giving me pause. Slowly, I turned to face her. The past between me and Shaunie was volatile, rocky. Toxic relationship? That was us. Until I ended it. It wasn't the fact that she was questioning me, it was the way she said "*her*" that tripped me out. Almost like she was jealous. And since I knew her to be a vindictive woman, I wanted to make it clear that Alaiya was off limits to her, too. "What did you say?" I challenged, my voice low. "You want to repeat that?"

Shaunie swallowed visibly. "I'm just sayin'," she murmured. "Please don't do this."

Technically, I *could* terminate her lease. Shaunie wasn't the biggest weed dealer in the community, but at first glance, I definitely had "just cause" to evict with all the visible drug paraphernalia at the crib.

"Are you really doing this?" she asked, worry lining her features. "You know I would've never let anything happen to her."

She looked sincere enough, but I could never tell with Shaunie. One minute, she was the nicest person in the room. The next she was a damn demon in disguise. At the same time, I knew she needed the spot. She had two little kids, who I hoped were with her mother right now. "Where are the boys?"

Shaunie blinked, obviously thrown off by the change of subject. "With my mom."

"Good." I let out a heavy sigh. "The noise complaints, the parties, the strange cars parked on the street … I could make you leave, but I won't. Today. But consider this a warning."

"Oh," she crossed her arms over her chest, "so you're too good for us now? Your brother is running for office, and you want to distance yourself from the hood politics?"

"I'll never forget where I came from. But I *will* protect my investment." I picked up the roach clip from the table and held it up. "I don't care who you are."

"You're acting like you don't smoke."

Shrugging, I tossed the metal into a small trashcan. "Maybe I'm just tired of your bullshit? The only reason you're still here is because of those boys. I want them to have a home. But don't try me."

Without another word, I stomped down the hallway to the main bedroom. I didn't need directions because I knew where it was. After all, I'd lived in the house when I was with Shaunie. Painted the walls, laid the floors, remodeled the bathrooms …

When I stopped in front of the door, I turned to find Shaunie watching me intently. She didn't speak, but the question was in her eyes. Eventually, though, she walked away shaking her head. Then, I let myself into the room.

I spotted her right away, splayed out on the mattress, face down. "Laiya," I called.

"Huh?" she grunted, then let out a whimper.

I stared down at her. I brushed a strand of hair from her face, then smoothed my thumb over her furrowed brow. It was the closest I'd ever gotten to her bare skin. Because it was rare that we touched each other at all. A brief hug every so often, but that was the extent of our physical contact. Her eyes were closed, and she looked like an angel. Like I'd just got a glimpse of Heaven.

"Hey." I nudged her. "I need you to wake up."

One eye popped open. "Spencer? It's you?"

I smiled. "Yeah, I'm here."

"You're here to save me?" she whispered.

"I should let your butt stay here," I teased. "I told you not to come."

She giggled. "And I told you not to tell me what to do."

Earlier that morning, I'd run into her at Luca's Coney Island. She'd mentioned going to the party, but I warned her against it. It had been a long time since I'd attended one of Shaunie's sets, but nothing ever changed. Loud music. Drinks. Drugs. Dancing. Fights. Good thing I got there before all hell broke loose.

With a heavy sigh, I picked her up, cradling her in my arms. She smelled like snow, so crisp, but slightly sweet. I wanted to bury my nose in her hair, in her neck. "Where's your purse?"

Curling into me, she mumbled, "I don't know. Probably out there." She frowned. "I think I gave it to Shaunie."

"How did you get here?"

"I drove."

*Shit.*

"Spence?" She lifted her head up, meeting my gaze. "Is it normal to not feel my face?"

"They don't call that bong *Lucifer* for no reason."

"Don't remind me. I couldn't stop coughing. I ate a whole box of Frosted Flakes."

Chuckling, I said, "That's a lot."

"I'm never doing this again," she promised.

"Good. Now, let's get you out of here."

As I carried her toward the front of the house, I asked Shaunie to bring me her purse and told O to make sure her car stayed where it was. When Fred opened the front door for me, Rodger Mills was standing there.

*Figures.*

He frowned. "What are you doing?"

"Taking her home."

Laiya lifted her head again. "Rod? What are you doing here?"

"I came to get you," he said. "Shaunie called me."

I whirled around to face Shaunie, but she wasn't quick enough to wipe that smirk off her face. She shrugged. "I figured her *man* should know what happened."

Rod held his arms out. "I'll take her."

"You should've been here with her," I snapped.

"I had to work," he explained unnecessarily. I didn't give a fuck about his excuses. "She's my girlfriend. *I* got her."

I glanced down at Laiya. For the first time tonight, her eyes were clear and locked on mine. "You want to go with him?" I asked.

Her eyes fluttered closed and her head fell against my shoulder. To any observer, they might've thought she was just high. But I knew her ... If she wanted to go with him, she would've made it more than clear.

"Laiya?" Rod called. "Come on."

Decision made, I looked at him. "Nah, man. I'll take her home. You can meet us there."

*Her Prologue*

**Alaiya**

*Twenty-Five Years Ago*

"I can't marry him."

Aunt Vicki eyed me curiously over the rim of her mug. "What did you just say?"

Truthfully? Most of my family wasn't shit. My mother was an addict who didn't stop having babies she couldn't support. My father was absent. I didn't even know his name, but I'd heard enough about him to thank God for that. My siblings—all ten of them—were either in jail, strung out, or hiding from their past.

I thought I was alone in this world, destined to do nothing with my life, doomed to repeat the mistakes that my mother made. Until Aunt Vicki found me. I was already an adult, working a part-time job at Hudson's Department Store while I took night classes at the community college. In a twist of fate, I ran into her at a makeup counter. She took one look at me and knew that I was related to her. It took a few minutes for her to convince me, but that day changed my life. I woke up that day by myself and fell asleep with an instant family, unwavering support from her and Uncle Linc, and so many cousins I couldn't remember their names at first. They'd been there every step of the way. They loved me. And now I needed her to tell me I wasn't making a huge mistake.

"Babe," Aunt Vicki placed her hand atop mine and squeezed, "I need you to talk to me. The wedding is in a week."

I glanced at the table next to us. We were seated at one of those quaint cafes on the University of Michigan campus. It was our thing. Lunch on Wednesdays. Just me and her. I stared at my plate. My appetite was gone, so I pushed it away. "I love him, but …"

I did love Rod. He was my very best friend, had been a huge part of my life. We'd met on campus, had taken the same introductory classes, went to the same events. We had comfortable companionship, a connection that ran deep. Not just physically, but emotionally. I knew he wouldn't treat me bad. He'd never hurt me. I felt safe with him. So when he told me he had feelings for me, I just went with it.

Aunt Vicki frowned. "You're not sure." It wasn't a question, but a statement.

I nodded. "It's just … When you met Uncle Stew, you knew that you wanted him."

She snickered. "Actually, I couldn't stand him."

My eyes widened. "Really?"

"Girl, everything he did got on my damn nerves."

Leaning forward, I asked, "When did it change?"

"It didn't take long, but one day I realized he was everything." She smiled to herself, almost as if she remembered something so sweet. "He protected me, even from myself. Back then, the family was in shambles. I wanted to get away from everything. He was my escape. He made time for me.

He wanted to hear about my day. Not to mention, he was so fine."

I chuckled. "Sometimes I feel like the family broke me." Everyone I loved had hurt me in ways I didn't think I could survive. The pain, the heartbreak made it hard to believe that I could ever be happy with anyone. "I have a hard time with trust."

"Do you trust Rodger?"

I nodded without hesitation. "He's a good guy. It's me."

"What's the problem?"

The bells above the front door jingled, signaling a patron entered the café. I glanced at the door, just as Spencer walked inside. His brother, Ryan, pointed toward the back of the building, and they made their way to an empty booth.

A nervous thrill ran down my spine as he headed toward us. Absently, I gripped the edge of the table, simultaneously wishing he wouldn't see me and hoping that he would. *He did.*

Spence stopped in his tracks when he noticed me. A corner of his mouth lifted. "What's up, Laiya?"

I schooled my features, glancing up at him. "Hey, Spence."

"Ryan?" Aunt Vicki said.

"Victoria Young." Ryan leaned down and gave my aunt a quick hug. "It's been too long. How's Stew?"

"He's good," she explained. "How's the family?"

"Great."

She introduced me. "This is my niece, Alaiya."

Ryan frowned. "I know Alaiya." He greeted me with a smile and a quick hug. Turning to my aunt, he asked, "How did I not know she was your niece?"

"Dort's daughter," Aunt Vicki explained.

I couldn't help but feel like lab specimen as Ryan searched my face. "Small world. Laiya lived on my mother's block for years."

Aunt Vicki leaned back, her eyes wide. "Wow."

While they chatted a few minutes about his upcoming campaign for mayor of Ypsilanti, Spence stared at me. Suddenly uncomfortable, I spent a few seconds smoothing my hands over the tablecloth, adjusting the salt-and-pepper shakers, and sipping my water. It had been months since he'd carried my high ass out of that house party, and I'd avoided contact with him since. Now I was forced to talk to him, to look at him, to acknowledge the way he always made me feel. Warm. Safe.

It had been that way since the first day I'd seen him. He'd given me his bologna sandwich because I was hungry. I had already moved at least ten times and attended five different elementary schools by my seventh birthday. That particular day, my mother had disappeared, leaving me at home with one of my "uncles". To protect myself, I'd left the house. It was hot outside, but my mother hadn't done laundry in weeks. I had no clean clothes, so I wore an old Halloween costume. Then, Spence came and sat with me until I had no choice but to go home.

He reached out and brushed my shoulder. It was an innocent touch, but I felt it in every part of my body. I peered over at Aunt Vicki, who was still talking to Ryan, before I turned back to Spence. "How's it going?"

"How are *you*?" he tossed back.

"Good," I lied. "Just working. School." I swallowed hard, then blurted out, "Rod proposed."

Spence's brows drew together. "You're engaged?"

My throat went dry. "Yes," I croaked.

"Were you engaged the last time I saw you?"

When I realized that the conversation had stopped on the other side of the table, I looked over at my aunt and Ryan. Sure enough, they were watching us.

After clearing my throat, I explained, "He asked me to marry him that morning, actually." And I'd been so caught off guard, so nervous, so scared, I went to that party. I wanted to escape—even if it was just for a little while. "We're going to have a small ceremony in Toledo next week."

"Why so fast?" he asked.

"Rod doesn't want to wait."

"What about what *you* want?"

I shot my aunt a sidelong glance. The look in her eyes told me she had the same question, so I told *both* of them, "This is what I want."

His jaw clenched. "I guess you know what you're doing. Ryan, I'm going to head to the table."

Ryan glanced at me, then Spence, and finally back at me. "Right. We better leave you two beautiful ladies to your lunch." He squeezed my hand. "Laiya, congrats on your engagement." He smiled at my aunt. "Vicki, tell Stew to give me a call."

"I will," Aunt Vicki assured, keeping her eyes trained on me.

A moment later, we were alone again. She didn't speak for what felt like an eternity, so I broke the ice. "I didn't realize you knew the Cross family."

Aunt Vicki followed my lead and answered, "We met years ago. Went to college together."

"I knew Spence was younger than his other siblings. I guess I just didn't think you'd know them."

"I grew up in Ypsi and I know a lot of people." Aunt Vicki had severed ties with most of the family, but it made sense that she still maintained a connection with some of the people she grew up with. "Linc and Ryan's brother were in the Navy together. So there's a history there."

"I bet. Did Uncle Stew grow up in Ypsi, too?"

"No. He's Ann Arbor through and through. But he hung out on the South Side occasionally. Which is how I met him. I thought he was my cousin since we had the same last name."

Cracking up, I asked, "I wondered about that."

"He had to convince me we weren't related. Not too many *Youngs* around here."

"It worked out, though. And you didn't have to change your last name."

"Exactly." She sipped her tea. "So, I wanted to give you a chance to get your bearings after that awkward encounter. Earlier, I asked you what the problem was between you and Rod. But the better question is … *who* is the problem?"

Unable to help myself, I glanced back at Spence. Not surprisingly, he was staring at me. I forced myself to turn away, to look at my aunt. "Spence is a friend. Innocent. We've known each other for years."

"Hm. Let me ask you … when you think about the man that you want to marry, the man that you would love to spend the rest of your life with … is it Rod?"

I blinked. "What? I-I don't … Why do ask that?"

"Because the way Spencer is looking at you and the way *you* reacted to Spencer? That's not innocent. And it certainly isn't just friends."

"Spence is not the guy for me."

"Why?"

I shrugged. "It's just not like that with us."

Aunt Vicki raised a questioning brow. "I don't want you to do anything that you'll regret, babe. Maybe take some time and think about it. Don't rush into marriage."

Although my aunt made valid points, I couldn't *not* marry Rod because of some silly crush I might have developed when Spence gave me his lunch all those years ago. Spence was nice looking. And he was kind. To me. He always looked out. For me. When he entered the room, people stopped what they were doing and started watching him.

Forget the way he held me in his arms.

Forget the way he'd marched me out of that damn house and dared everyone there to say something.

Forget the feel of his breath against my neck as he buckled me into his car.

Definitely forget the heat of his eyes on mine that night. And today.

*Forget the damn flutters, Laiya.*

I sat up straight, tugged at my shirt. "Aunt Vicki, I understand your concern. But I know what I want."

"Do you? Because earlier you said you can't get married."

Waving a dismissive hand her way, I said, "I was mistaken. Wedding jitters. I'm going to marry Rod." I swallowed past a hard lump in my throat. "It's what I want."

*And if I keep repeating it, maybe I'll believe it.*

# CHAPTER 1

*Grown & Sexy*

**Spencer**

*Present Day*

I should've known it was a setup.

From the moment I'd arrived at the Smoke and Burn Lounge, I felt uneasy. Like I'd walked into a trap. The beginning chords of the Temptations classic, "Silent Night," played over the speaker. Soon, Dennis Edwards sang the magic words, *"In my mind."* Around me, several women raised their hands in appreciation while the few men there nodded their heads to the slow melody.

A stray flyer on an empty table confirmed my initial thought. I picked the thick cardstock up and studied it. The low-lit, chill nightspot had been transformed into a weird-ass Christmas-themed matchmaking event. The Mistletoe Match.

As I made my way toward the bar, a few random women stopped me to ask if I was there to be matched. To my right, a young woman winked at me. Another lady flashed a bright smile when I passed by her table.

And here I was thinking, *What the hell am I doing here?*

"Uncle!" My niece, Taylar, approached me, a huge smile on her face. "You made it." She gave me a hug and clapped. "I'm so happy."

Narrowing my eyes, I asked, "What did you get me into, Tay?"

"I told you, it's our annual speed-dating event."

"Yeah, nah." I gripped my coat when she tried to take it from me. "I'm not doing this."

Taylar's shoulders fell. "Please, stay," she begged, finally winning the tug-of-war with me.

*Only because I let her.*

"What's up, Unc?" My nephew, Ryker, gave me a dap and set a bottle of my favorite beer on the bar top. "Figured you'd need this."

I took a sip. "Why am I here, Jellybean?" She opened her mouth to speak, but I rushed on, "I don't want the business-woman explanation. I want the truth."

"It's a night out. Free food. Potential hook up." She hunched a shoulder. "Besides, you're a good catch." She blew out a frustrated breath. "Based on the feedback from last year, we were missing one key demographic."

Eyeing Taylar, I asked, "What's that?"

She scratched the back of her neck. "Zaddy," she grumbled.

Ryker barked out a laugh. "I believe she's calling you old, Unc."

"Shut up." Taylar glared at her big brother. She pointed at the woman who just walked to the bar. "Go help that lady." Once Ryker walked away, she turned to me. "You're not old, Uncle Spencie. Just mature. We have some amazing boss-women who aren't interested in that Cougar Life."

I never had kids of my own, never really wanted to be a

father, but I was a damn good uncle. And my niece—the only person on earth that could call me "Spencie" and get away with it—always managed to talk me into some bullshit. "Fine. I'll stay. For a little while."

Taylar beamed. "Thank you," she whispered. For the next few minutes, she explained to me the process. Based on a profile she'd created for me, I would be matched with four different women. The goal was to talk, get to know each other, then decide if we want to take it to the next level. Seemed easy enough.

"How did you come up with these matches?" I asked.

"You remember my friend, Bliss, right?"

I nodded. "Yeah."

"She's the matchmaker. We've been doing this for several years now. I've already planned five weddings for past attendees."

"You do realize I'm not going to be number six?"

"Of course, Uncle." She led me over to a table near the front of the cigar lounge. "You're at Table five. I'll send your first date over."


"WHAT EXACTLY IS a bud and breakfast anyway?"

From across the room, I noticed Taylar and Bliss watching the scene unfold. My niece motioned at me, urging me with her hands and eyes to talk to my "date".

"Hello?" the woman across from me pressed, a scowl on her face. From the moment she'd arrived, she'd commanded attention from the fellas. Lovely body. Check. Full lips. Check. Smooth, brown skin. Check. Foul attitude. *Nah, I'm good.*

"Yes?" I answered finally, not giving a damn if the boredom on my face was obvious.

"What is a bud and breakfast?" she asked again, brow furrowed.

She was the third woman to join me at my table. The first

one was pleasant enough, but she wanted a wedding ring. The second match ... Well, we didn't make it the full half hour before she asked me to invest in her home health care business. She also wanted to walk down that aisle. I had already been someone's husband, and I wasn't interested in a repeat performance. My ex-wife had made my life miserable for five years. Not enough sex. Too much nagging. Every day fights. Lofty expectations that only applied to me, never her.

"Mr. Cross? Hello?" Third Date called again dramatically.

Ignoring her, I picked up my phone and sent a quick text to my niece:

> Ask Bliss why she's torturing me. And what the hell is this woman's name?

It took a few seconds, but Taylar finally responded:

> Yolanda. Can you at least try to act interested?

Leaning back in my chair, I shifted my attention back to the woman across from me. "A *bud* and breakfast is like a *bed* and breakfast, except it's cannabis friendly. We're a smaller establishment, on private property. Our guests enjoy the freedom to indulge whether its smoking, vaping, or eating marijuana. Legally. We provide cannabis-infused meals, a complimentary weed bar with several strains, and smoking implements."

It was a spiel I'd memorized for people like her, a log line of sorts. Usually, I was met with two very specific responses—judgement or intrigue. More times than not, I walked away with a booking, but sometimes I encountered undercover church ladies disguised as progressive.

"Is that all you do?" The judgement in her tone made me want to get up. "Because ..." she shrugged, "that doesn't seem like a lucrative business. Seems more like a little hobby to me. What exactly do you do all day anyway? Smoke weed with your guests?"

"Am I supposed to take that as a serious question?" I asked.

"I'm sorry," she said softly, tracing her finger over the small plate on the table. "Maybe we got off on the wrong foot? I'm just ... nervous. I've never done anything like this before."

Rubbing my beard, I counted to ten slowly. *Ten more minutes.* "Can I ask what you do?"

Her shoulders fell, and I figured I'd hit a nerve. "I work for my father." She scratched the back of her neck. "He's the senior pastor of Ram in the Bush Tabernacle. You might know him. Bishop Floyd Matthews."

Suddenly, everything made sense. Looking at her, though, I wouldn't exactly classify her as an undercover church lady. More like an entitled, pampered princess who didn't think twice about using her last name or her father's standing in the community to demean others she deemed beneath her. She was the exact type of woman I'd avoided at all costs. I'd met a few of those throughout my life. Had family members that behaved that way, too. "Ah."

"What is that supposed to mean?" She folded her arms across her chest. "Are you judging me?"

I raised a brow. "Like you judged me?"

She rolled her eyes. "I wasn't judging you. I don't even drink alcohol, so I know next to nothing about marijuana. The Bible implores us to be sober-minded."

"1 Peter 5:8. I know scripture. I know your father, too."

Ole' Floyd was the poster boy for "once was blind but now I see." The fact that people in our old hood seemed to gloss over the fact that he was once the biggest drug dealer in our hometown of Ypsilanti, Michigan was comical. But I would never forget the havoc he caused, and all the lives ruined by his quest for money. Knowing Yolanda was the bishop's daughter only further cemented that this was no match made in Heaven.

"And, yes, you were judging me," I added. "You've made assumptions about me from the moment I told you about my business."

"I didn't mean to come off that way," she said. "I'm—"

"I know. You're sorry." I dropped a twenty-dollar bill on the table for the waitress, then finished my beer. It was my second one in the last hour, not nearly strong enough to deal with this bullshit. Before I could make my hasty exit, though, my phone buzzed. I glanced at the screen, then at Taylar, who seemed to understand that I was hanging on by a thin string.

TAY

Please don't get up and walk away like you did the last woman.

TAY

I have done several weddings at her father's church.

TAY

Come on, Uncle Spencie. This is my business. Don't be mean.

"I do apologize." Yolanda shifted in her chair, drawing my attention back to her. "So you own a weed business?"

"Actually, I have two," I corrected, chuckling when she tried—and failed—to school her face. "Both are part of an expansive real estate portfolio."

She perked up then, batting her eyelashes and leaning a little closer. Her scowl turned into what I assumed was her version of a seductive smile. "Oh, that's interesting."

Amazing how her tone changed once she thought I had some money. Only a few minutes ago, she was ready to douse me in Holy Water and banish me to the altar for my sins.

After the not-so-subtle shade she'd thrown, I could've taken the opportunity to make her feel like shit by revealing how her father had embezzled money from his church for years and scammed his parishioners out of thousands of their hard-earned dollars so he could purchase a private jet. I wasn't an asshole, though. At least, not regularly. And only if I cared enough to expend that type of energy. In this case, she didn't matter enough to go there.

Time seemed to stretch on as Yolanda babbled on about residential and commercial real estate. She didn't seem to notice that I hadn't said a word in the last few minutes. I scanned the room, looking for my niece, recognizing several faces from around the way. While some seemed excited to be there, most were undoubtedly counting the minutes until this event was over.

I fired off another text to my niece:

> My time is up. I'm out.

Taylar emerged from the back of the building just as the song switched to another old school Christmas classic. But my niece didn't come save me. Instead, she walked toward the front door to greet another group of women as they entered the lounge. A familiar set of brown eyes locked on mine, and curiosity eclipsed my need to leave in that moment.

Across from me, Yolanda sang along to the song playing through the speakers. She wasn't the only one either. Apparently, being lonely at Christmas resonated to a lot of the attendees. But my attention was firmly on the woman now exchanging hugs with Tay.

"My father has several homes on the south side that he rents out to his parishioners," Yolanda boasted. "He's considered one of the leaders of the community because of his contributions. How do you know him?"

I couldn't even pretend to care about this conversation anymore. I stood up. "He used to sell crack on our block. Tonight was … an experience. Drive safe. Merry Christmas."

My original plan was to slip outside while Taylar was preoccupied with other guests, but as I approached the bar, Yolanda caught up with me. "Wait." She grabbed my arm. "You can't just accuse my father of being a drug dealer and—"

"Hi, Yolanda." Bliss appeared behind me, clipboard in hand and a bright smile on her face.

*Where the hell did she come from*?

Yolanda sputtered, "Um … Hi. Do I know you?"

"I'm one of the organizers of the event. We spoke on the phone the other day?"

"Oh." Yolanda nodded. "I remember now. Ms. Young?"

"Exactly. Can I talk to you for a minute?" Bliss asked. "There was a problem with your registration."

Without another word, Yolanda followed Bliss to the table near the door. Taking that as my cue, I headed toward the back of the building where Taylar was waiting with my coat.

Taylar approached me. "I had a fourth date for you, ya know?"

Sighing, I kissed her brow. "I tried, Jellybean. Yolanda Matthews was the last straw."

"My bad, Uncle Spencie. Bliss just told her to leave. She lied on her registration form. Apparently, she has three young kids. But on her profile, she indicated that she had no children. Who does that?"

I let out a humorless chuckle. "I guess she's more like her father than I thought," I murmured.

Taylar offered me a sad smile. "This event was a bust. Ryker had to break up a fight in the bathroom. Someone's wife signed up to be matched and got caught."

My protective instinct kicked in. "Do you need me to handle it?" Because I would—*and have*—beat the shit out of anyone who fucked with my family. It wasn't that long ago that I almost got arrested climbing into a window to get my sister's daughter out of some dusty-ass nigga's house. Much to the chagrin of my brother, who was running a re-election campaign defending his state office during that time. I didn't give a damn though.

Shaking her head, she said, "No. Keon and Ryker handled it."

"Good." For the most part, I didn't have to worry about Taylar. Ryker and Maddox took their big brother roles very seriously. And she was currently engaged to Keon Webb, who I'd known since he was a kid. Standup guy. I knew he would protect her with his life.

"We're going to have to rebrand next year, though," she admitted, finally giving me my coat.

I pulled her into a tight hug. "I have no doubt you'll figure everything out."

From the time Jellybean was born, she'd been a force to be reckoned with. She'd exceeded expectations in school, at work, and now as the owner of Taylar Made Events. Even without the approval of my brother, she left corporate America behind to invest in herself. And because I'd always encouraged her to take those leaps of faith, I'd invested in her as well. Looking at her now, I couldn't be more proud of her.

"Do you mind staying a little longer?" she asked. "Bliss and I would love to get your feedback. Plus, I just miss you. I haven't seen you in a minute." I eyed her skeptically, and she cracked up. "I promise I won't try to set you up again."

"Alright. I'll stick around. But don't play me."

Taylar disappeared again once I took a seat at the bar. She returned a few minutes later with a plate of food and set the meal in front of me. "Eat. We have so much food in the back. I don't want it to go to waste. Shoot." She snapped. "I forgot the cornbread."

"I got him." I turned toward the voice and was met with

the knowing eyes of Alaiya Young. Taylor dashed off, leaving me with the woman who'd distracted me from the moment she'd walked in earlier. She handed me a small saucer with two pieces of buttery cornbread on top and took a seat on the empty barstool next to me. "I figured you'd want two."

Chuckling, I said, "Thanks, Laiya."

Alaiya jumped up. "Oh shit. I forgot the hot sauce."

In her haste to leave, she dropped a piece of paper on the floor. Bending down, I picked it up. I didn't intend on reading it, but the title caught my attention.

ALAIYA'S MOVE-THE-FUCK-ON PLAN

1. GET MONEY (NO PROBLEMS)

2. PURGE

3. EDIBLES / DRINKS

4. A NIGGA (PREFERABLY WITH A LONG, HARD DICK)

5. VIBES

"I'm back." Alaiya handed me a bottle of hot sauce. "I need to get in shape for real." She blew out a deep breath, muttered a curse, and sat back down. "I'm telling you, I—" She froze, her brow furrowed. "What?"

I blinked. "Huh?"

"You're staring."

*Shit.* I probably was staring at her. For some reason, I couldn't tear my gaze away from her tonight. From the moment she'd walked in earlier, I was officially transfixed by her presence. Almost as if I'd never laid eyes on her before. Which was surprising since I'd just spent the afternoon with her a couple of days ago. Had breakfast with her last week. After all, she was my real estate agent, and we were set to close on a new property in a matter of days. Not to mention, her daughter, Desiree, worked for me.

Unlike most of the women in the space, Alaiya wasn't wearing gold glitter or red. Her modern black suit was simple, yet elegant. Her short hair was styled to perfection, her makeup natural. She was stunning. Lovely. *As always.*

Obviously, I was missing something very important because … *that list.* We'd never had a problem communicating, but I also didn't want to be all up in her business either. My curiosity was killing me, though.

"Spence?" she called softly.

I shook my head out of my thoughts. Clearing my throat, I muttered, "I'm sorry. Distracted."

"Are you okay?"

"I'm fine," I assured her. "What's going on with you?"

Alaiya spun around in the barstool and stared out the picture window. "Nothing much."

Time and experience had shaped her, but she was still the same person I met on the neighborhood playground when I was ten years old—minus the big braids in her hair and Wonder Woman costume on. I remembered because it wasn't Halloween, and it was hot as hell at the park that day. *Too* hot for that plastic mask and outfit. I also couldn't forget the despair written on her face, the tears in her eyes. That day, she was tired, hungry, and alone. Although I was only three years older than her, it didn't sit right with me. Even now, her eyes told the story she probably didn't want to share.

And tonight … List aside, something was off.

"You good?" I asked.

Tilting her head from side to side, she nibbled on her bottom lip as if she was weighing her words carefully. She flashed a soft smile, but it didn't reach her eyes. Yet, she still answered, "I am."

*She's lying.*

"I have a question for you, though," she said.

In that moment, I made the decision to follow her lead and accept what she said as her truth. I needed to focus on my food and not on her emotions … or her list. Because I couldn't afford to get lost in her. Been there. Done that. *She* was none of my damn business anymore.

I scooped up some mac and cheese. "What's up?"

"What are you doing here?" She drummed her fingernails on the bar top.

I ate another steak tip and tipped my head toward Taylar, who was still making her rounds. "You already know."

Alaiya nodded. "Say less. Taylar is definitely a boss."

"Boss-*y*," I corrected.

"You couldn't have said no?"

I shrugged. "Maybe. But she's had me wrapped around her finger since she flashed that first toothless grin in my direction."

"That's cute." She stared at me. Through me, really. "I guess I won't judge you then."

I smirked. "Was that where this was going?"

"I don't know," she mused.

"Taylar wanted a more mature crowd," I explained between bites. "Tried to convince me to take a chance."

Her face lit up finally, and she giggled. "You must be the *Zaddy* I heard about."

Now, that smile? *Fuck*. It was blinding, really. Breathtaking. And again, I was spellbound, captivated by her.

*Or I'm losing my mind.*

She leaned back, searching my face. "I can see why they think that."

For a brief moment, I stared into those expressive dark brown eyes before my gaze dropped to the curve of her nose, then finally her mouth. "Can you?"

Clearing her throat, she looked away and smoothed her hands over her lap. "Of course. Reminds me of back in the day. All the girls on the block chasing after you."

"They didn't catch me, though," I joked.

"If I recall, some of them did. I still remember Shaunie walking down the middle of the street with that bat, threatening to set KiKi's house on fire for daring to speak to you at the bowling alley."

I groaned. "That was a hot-ass mess," I agreed. Shaunie

was a lifetime ago. It had taken a while, but she'd finally met and married some guy from Texas. She'd been living down south for a decade. "I never fucked with KiKi."

"Sure?" she asked, lifting a questioning brow. "'Cause the streets were talking."

Waving a dismissive hand her way, I grumbled, "Yeah. Always making up bullshit." I forced myself to focus on my plate again. I bit into my last tender steak tip. "This was good as hell."

Alaiya flashed a satisfied grin. "Des did her thing, huh?"

An overwhelming sense of pride shot through me at her admission and a smile tugged at my lips. "On her own?" I asked.

Alaiya was a devoted, dedicated mother to her only daughter, Desiree. It was obvious that she'd raised a capable, talented, intelligent young woman who'd also become a valuable part of my team. "Des" had worked her way up from part-time employee to manager of two of my properties. Her innovative ideas had been integral to my bottom line. Recently, she'd been added to my rotation of chefs responsible for curating cannabis-infused breakfast at each of The Leaf Lodge locations. I trusted her with my business, but I also encouraged her to follow her own dreams. And it wasn't that long ago that she'd come to me, business plan in hand, asking for my input on her new catering business.

"With a little help from my cousin," Alaiya replied. "Duke helped her with the menu and helped her shop. He also played sous chef today."

I glanced at the entrance to the kitchen. "Is she still here?"

"You know she's a perfectionist." She sighed. "She won't come out. Keeps insisting she's where she needs to be."

"Tell her I need her to bring me a pan of this cornbread to work tomorrow." I bit into a piece. It tasted more like dessert than bread—soft, moist, and buttery.

She scratched the back of her neck. "That was actually

me." She held her finger up to her mouth. "My contribution to the evening."

I eyed her out of the corner of my eye. *Damn*. In all the years I'd known her, I couldn't say that I'd ever eaten anything she'd cooked. Probably because I made sure to keep our interactions cordial, professional … distant. That didn't mean I never wanted something more. Alaiya was a beautiful woman. We had a natural connection, but she was off-limits to me. And I had to be good with that.

Shrugging, she said, "I'll wrap you up a few pieces to take home." She smiled at Ryker when he set a glass of water in front of her. Then, she glanced around the room. "Look at this. See that woman over there?" She pointed to my left. "With the silver glitter jumpsuit?"

I easily found the woman in the crowd. She was smiling from ear-to-ear, speaking in an outside voice. "You know her?"

Alaiya shook her head. "Yeah. I used to work with her at Hudsons."

"That's a long time ago."

"Right? Anyway, she confessed to me that she's hoping to find her fifth husband tonight. But she also said that she still hadn't left her fourth husband." She sighed. "I understand why people sign up for stuff like this, but I don't trust it. People lie. They act good when they're bad. Pretend to have money when they're broke. Everyone is simply presenting the image they think someone would be attracted to. Like Yolanda."

Tilting my head to the side, I waited for her to elaborate. When she didn't, I pressed her. "*What* about Yolanda?"

"I caught a glimpse of her profile."

The pieces started to click together. "You just happened to see it?"

She cracked up. "Man, you know I looked at that shit on purpose."

Chuckling, I teased, "Glad you cleared that up."

"Anyway, I saw that you could use an assist, so I pulled Taylar to the side and told her what's up."

I held up my fist. "Good lookin' out."

She bumped hers with mine. "No problem."

My eyes locked on hers. This time she didn't look away. "You don't like her."

"Can't stand her," she admitted. "Or her daddy."

My mind swirled with so many questions. I knew the bishop because I was twenty years younger than my oldest sibling and I'd seen with my own eyes the way he used to be out in these streets. Alaiya was only a few years younger than me, though. I wondered about her connection to that family. "How do you know them so well?"

"Church," she grumbled. "My aunt used to drag me to Sunday school. Let's just say, several people in my family were once clients of Bishop Matthews back in the day. And I know for a fact that he didn't stop dealing after he became the associate pastor of that church."

"And Yolanda? What did she do?"

She shrugged. "She's just a bitch."

I barked out a laugh. "You're silly."

"Anyway, it was either tell Taylar the truth, or ask to be your next date. Full disclosure—I was leaning toward the date idea." She flashed a devious smirk. "Only because I knew it would piss Yolanda off."

Now I had one more question. And a confession. Leaning closer, I whispered, "As long as we're being honest, you could've been my final date tonight. I would've had no problem spending the rest of the evening with you. But ..." my gaze dropped to her mouth, "I imagine that would be a problem for your husband." I slid the list over to her, and her eyes widened. "Right?"

# CHAPTER 2
## On and On

*Alaiya*

Obviously, I fucked up. *Or I'm just fucked.*

It made sense when I made my list. I felt better afterward, too. Especially after that muthafucka stole my money. Instead of revenge, I just wanted to move the fuck on.

I *wanted* access to my bank account.

I *wanted* an empty house.

I *wanted* to forget.

I *wanted* to get fucked.

I *wanted* peace. *And* fun. *And* laughter. *And* positive energy.

The last thing I *wanted* was to drop my private list in a public bar. The absolute worst thing that could've happened did. Spencer Cross just happened to find it. Any doubt I had that he read the entire list was miniscule, because he absolutely read that shit. Just the thought … I swallowed as a wave of nausea passed over me. I flattened a hand on my stomach.

*I'm gonna be sick.*

"Laiya?"

Tonight wasn't supposed to go like this. I'd done a good job of compartmentalizing my life—and the people in it. Spence was a good person. Dependable. Loyal. Honest. Kind. He was so much more, but mostly, he was respectful. He'd never inserted himself in my business. Until now. *Is that what this is, though*?

Letting out a slow breath, I finally answered, "Yes?"

"Are you okay?"

My vision blurred as tears threatened to fall. I closed my eyes, willing myself to pull it together. Then, I felt it. Soft Kleenex against my skin, warm fingers brushing my cheek as he wiped my face.

"I'm sorry," I whispered.

He wrapped his arms around my waist. "Come on. Let's get you out of here."

It felt like déjà vu because we *had* been here before. The first time I'd met him, he'd offered me comfort and his bologna sandwich. And so many times after that. All the way up until I married Rod. Now, he was leading me away from the fray so that I wouldn't lose all my damn cool points in the middle of the Smoke and Burn Cigar Lounge.

"Your food," I said lamely as I followed him up the staircase in the back of the restaurant. "You didn't finish your mac and cheese."

"Don't worry about me."

We stopped in front of a door. He unlocked it and gently pulled me inside. Once he flipped the light switch, I realized we were in an apartment.

"Is this …"

"The plan was to turn this into a short-term rental, but the fellas decided to keep it empty for now." He walked to the fridge and pulled out two bottles of water and a fifth of tequila. "Works out because sometimes they stay here after a long night."

"And why do you have a key?"

"Ryker offered it to me."

Something told me there was more to the story, and I decided to toss out my suspicion. "Because you helped him get the building?"

He chuckled. "Silent partner."

"Not surprised." I wasn't shocked he didn't lead with that either. He rarely boasted about his success.

Spence had emerged as a leader in our neighborhood right around his freshman year in high school. He'd complained about the lack of investment in the Black community from city and township officials and swore he would make changes once he had the resources. When Ryan ran for mayor, I'd assumed Spence would follow in his footsteps eventually.

Except for a minor stint in city council, Spence had chosen to stay away from politics, though. Instead, he'd received his undergraduate degree in finance and worked in commercial banking before he left his corporate job and created Cross Investments. He'd amassed an impressive real estate portfolio before he segued into hospitality. But he'd also taught classes on entrepreneurship and had even assisted in the development of several small businesses in the area.

I scanned the living room. It was nice, really. Clean. Grey walls, wood floors, a small sectional in the corner, and a little table near the kitchen. Taking a seat, I watched him grab two shot glasses from the cabinet.

"It's comfortable in here. Quiet, considering there's a whole party downstairs."

He winked. "The magic of good insulation."

After he took a seat next to me, he handed me a bottle of water and set the liquor and the shot glasses on a table in front of the couch. We didn't speak for a moment, and I suspected he was waiting on me to set the tone.

I pointed to the tequila. "You know I don't drink that stuff."

A smirk played on his lips, and he shrugged. "I figured you might want to try something different, especially since you mentioned needing a drink."

I hung my head. "So, you *did* read it?"

"Yeah," he confessed.

I eyed him skeptically. "Why?"

He rubbed the side of his face. "Honestly, it was the most exciting discovery of the night."

Cracking up then, I fell back on the cushion. My chest expanded as the heaviness I'd felt only seconds earlier vanished. "I can't believe you." I shoved him playfully and tucked my legs under my bottom. "Really?"

He rested his back against the sofa, turning his head toward me. "Actually, there were two things. That food *and* your move-the-fuck on plan."

"Why?"

"Because your list ..." He hunched a shoulder. "I understand the money thing. We all need a little more. But you don't drink, though."

"I do," I argued. "I love wine and daiquiris. And mojitos. Oh, and I tried some of that Mike's Hard last summer." His mouth curved into a smile, but I chose to ignore how that one action made me question us being alone. "You want to laugh at me, don't you?"

He raised his hands up. "No, I wouldn't laugh at you."

For some reason, his words made me feel centered again. Because he'd never made fun of me. Even when other kids used to crack jokes at my expense. He'd always had my back.

I brushed my thumb over the edge of the cushion. "Thanks."

"I also remember you swearing to God that would never try weed again."

My mouth fell open, and I shoved him playfully. "No, I said I'd never *smoke* weed again. And you know why?"

He barked out a laugh and, for some very strange reason, I wanted to climb into his lap and burrow into him. Everything about him—from his spicy, woody scent to his sincere eyes to the warmth emanating from him—made me want to stay here, hidden away from all my problems. Let's be real, Spence was sexy as hell. When we were younger, he was cute and all. *Okay, he's fine as fuck.* However, fifty-leven other girls around the way thought so, too.

But Grown Man Spence? With his salt-and-pepper beard, taper fade, smooth, brown skin, cut arms and stomach … I blinked myself out of my thoughts. Because, no. *I can't go there.* I snuck a look at him out of the corner of my eye and found him staring at me intently. Again.

*Lord.* He had a way of seeing me. It almost felt like he was looking into my soul. *Shit, can I go there?*

I feigned a cough, squared my shoulders, then steered the conversation back to the safe zone. "After that experience with Lucifer, I never want to *inhale* that shit again."

A smirk pulled at his lips. "Yeah, you were lit."

I smacked my palms against my thighs. "For days."

Unbeknownst to me at the time, a four-foot bong was not for play play. I learned that hard lesson as soon as I took a single hit and immediately started drooling all over myself. I was so high I could barely see. And hungry. I ate an entire box of cereal, promptly passed out, then had to be *carried* out by Spence. It took days to feel normal after that.

"I warned you."

Of course he did. In the *Spence* way. Voice low, eyes sincere. But I was no punk. He wasn't going to tell me what to do. I lived to regret that decision, though, hence the promise I made to myself to never smoke again.

"Matter of fact, let's not even talk about this. I've moved all the way past those years. Anyway, life has been life-ing. I have days when I'm more anxious than calm. Clients been getting on my nerves. I seriously considered closing my business without a plan. My homegirl suggested I try edibles."

"Damn, that's deep."

"Tell me about it."

"But you …" He shook his head "Never mind."

"What were you going to say?" I prodded.

"It's not appropriate. And we've already established that you don't listen to me."

"Don't play me," I admonished. "Please. You've always been honest, so tell me."

He squeezed my thigh. Look, I know it was an innocent gesture of comfort, I know I should've been paying attention to what he was saying, but I couldn't take my eyes off his hand on my thigh. Or keep my mind on the conversation and not on the way he'd practically seared my pant-covered skin with the contact. And when he finally pulled away, I missed the warmth of his touch.

"Laiya?"

I tore my gaze away from my leg, nibbling on my bottom lip. "Huh?"

"I hate that I didn't know you were going through something." He brushed a piece of hair from my face.

*I wonder if he realizes he's touching me.* I shifted away from him. "Spence, you know we don't talk about stuff like this."

"Why is that?"

"Because I—" I let out a nervous laugh. "Shit, I don't know. It's just the way things are."

While Spence and I grew up in the same neighborhood, we had completely different experiences. The Cross family was a beacon of light in the community. My home was a bottomless pit of hell. He had supportive parents and I had …

my shitty siblings, my no-good uncle, my holier-than-thou aunt, and my mother.

"We're cool," I explained. "Talking about our problems is not the nature of our relationship."

"Point taken," he agreed. "But it wasn't always like that."

I averted my gaze. There was one brief moment, before I married my soon-to-be ex, when I found myself so attracted, so drawn to Spence that I wanted to explore it. For a while, I could've sworn he'd felt the same way, but I never had the guts to voice it aloud. Then I married Rod. "We can't talk about that either."

He bumped my shoulder with his. "A 'nigga and vibes'? Can we talk about that?"

Leaning forward, I picked up the shot glass he'd just filled and took it. "Shit," I hissed, holding my throat. "Ugh. That's nasty."

We sat in silence for a moment.

"This is hard."

"What's hard?" he asked.

I figured the best place to start was the truth. "I filed for divorce last week." Taking another deep breath, I turned to him. "I married my best friend. I thought that would be enough to sustain us. For a while, it did. Even when we didn't see eye to eye on how we should run our household, we could still fall back on that genuine friendship. But when Rod turned forty-five, things shifted. He's always worked long hours, but he was barely home. And even when he was there, he didn't engage with us. With me. I don't even recognize him anymore. He's distant. Nasty, sometimes. Mean."

Spence sat up straight. "Is he violent?"

I placed my hand on his balled-up fist. "No." I shook my head for emphasis. "Never. But, Spence, he treats me like an at-will employee sometimes. I'm supposed to devote all my time and energy to him, cater to him, have sex with him ... He isn't interested in making me a priority in his life. His priority is his career, his parents, and his vices. And I can't take it anymore."

"What the fuck?"

The part of me that always defended my husband had died when he let his mother borrow ten racks for a cosmetic procedure without asking me.

"And then he …" My shoulders fell as resignation took over. I didn't bother wiping away the tear that escaped, but I did pay an extraordinary amount of attention to the way it slowly drizzled down my arm before it stopped. I'd spent years pretending to be happy, faking smiles, throwing dinner parties, putting his needs above all else. Over the years, I'd ignored *me* so that I could be everything to him. *And I'm tired.* Closing my eyes, I let more fall as I cried silently for the dissolution of my marriage.

Spence smoothed a hand over my back. "Laiya, what did he do?"

"Blew up. Destroyed some shit in the house, called me out my name, accused me of abandoning him so I could fuck some other nigga. Then, he drained our joint accounts, the savings that *I* worked on alone. The worst part? I was so sure that he would calm down and remember who we once were to each other that I didn't look out for myself. How could I be so stupid?"

He wrapped his arms around me, pulling me to him. "It's fucked up, Laiya. But you're going to be okay."

I dashed a fresh tear away from my cheek. "I don't even know why I'm crying. I have my own accounts. It's not like I can't support myself." I swallowed rapidly against the hard lump that had formed in my throat. "I just … It feels like a death."

"You love him."

I peered at him, searched his eyes. "I do love him. He's the father of my daughter. He was my best friend. But if I'm being honest with myself, I haven't been in love with Rod in years. We haven't slept in the same room in months. He has a girlfriend."

Frowning, he asked, "Did he tell you that?"

"I met her," I deadpanned. "He brought the bitch to my house yesterday, to get me to react. She works with him. I'm not stupid. He's been messing around with her since I kicked him out of our bedroom. Probably even before that."

"He's a fool, Laiya."

Rod was many things—hardworking, consistent, selfish, aloof—but 'a fool' wasn't one of them. "You have to say that because we're cool. And you hate Rod."

Spence chuckled. "I don't typically say things I don't mean. You know that."

"I remember when I told you I was getting married."

He dropped his head, rubbed his jaw. "Yeah. I do, too."

The look on Spence's face … I could never forget it. The memory had been seared on my brain so tough, I'd dreamed of that moment for years, analyzing what it could've meant. Even though my heart already knew.

"You were right," I admitted.

His eyes flashed to mine. "Don't do that." He shook his head. "You made the decision that you thought was right for you. You had a life with him. Years together. Divorce doesn't erase that."

"But what would've happened if I'd made a different choice?"

"Then you," he whispered, his gaze dropping to my mouth, "wouldn't have Des."

I squeezed my eyes shut, silently chastising myself for even voicing my thoughts out loud. Especially since my greatest accomplishment was being Desiree's mother. "She's pretty amazing, huh?"

"Exceptional," he agreed.

"I should probably go." I tried to get up, but his hand on my arm prevented me from standing. "I have an early showing. When I came here tonight, the plan was to try to forget. It wasn't supposed to be like this, me crying on your shoulder. And you letting me."

He brushed his thumb over my bottom lip and leaned in. "Even all these years later, I can't stop wanting to protect you. I can't make myself walk away from you."

I gripped his biceps, dug my fingernails into his flesh. "Spence, I—"

Maybe it was the fact that we were so close I could smell the tequila on his breath? Or it could've been because I hadn't been touched this way in months. Years. Not to mention I'd imagined this moment too many times to count. But my body was on fire, my heart was pounding in my ears, and I wanted him to close the distance. I wanted him to finally claim me.

"Don't worry," he circled my nose with his, "I'm not going to kiss you."

*Why*? The question was on the tip of my tongue, but I wouldn't voice it. I couldn't cross the line.

"I want to, though," he added, nipping my earlobe.

*Oh God.*

He stood then, taking his warmth with him. I blinked against the haze, tried to focus on anything but the desire coursing through my veins. Reaching out to me, he said, "But you're right. You should probably go."

I nodded. "Right," I croaked, slipping my hand in his and letting him pull me to my feet. "I have to check in on Des."

Spence's tongue darted out to lick his lips. "Laiya," he whispered.

"Yes?"

"We should talk soon," he suggested.

"Definitely."

"I have business I want to discuss with you."

In light of my current financial situation, I should've been elated with the prospect of new business, but I felt disappointed. Part of me hoped he'd want to discuss what just happened. *Or what could happen.*

"Sure."

"Among other things," he continued, much to my heart and body's content. Because the flutters were back in full force. "I usually don't put myself out there like this, but I feel like I should be honest. Make no mistake, I want to do more than kiss you. I want to strip you bare and take my time exploring every part of you." He took a step back. "You're still married, though. You're grieving a long-term relationship. I have to respect that. I won't insert myself into that process. However, I made a choice twenty-five years ago, too. I won't make the same mistake twice. Just so you know … all bets are off once that divorce decree is final." A smirk formed on his lips. "And I plan to cross off every item on that move-the-fuck-on list."

# CHAPTER 3
*I'll Be There for You*

*Spencer*

"**D**id you get my calls?"

"Is this a trick question?" I asked my sister when she waltzed into my office. After the tenth message, I'd placed my phone on DO NOT DISTURB. Because Sabrina didn't want anything. There was never an emergency. Somehow, she'd concluded that everyone needed to drop everything when she had an idea. This time, she'd solicited donations for the annual Jack and Jill Club Debutante Ball in April. When no one responded, she'd proceeded to badger us —in age order—until they relented and agreed to support the endeavor. It was my turn.

Sabrina took a seat across from my desk. "Ryan agreed to attend, so did Mark. All that leaves is you. We'd love to have Cross Investments sponsor one of the debutantes. Can I put you down to hold an entrepreneurship workshop?"

Ignoring her, I clicked through my emails. My morning had been jam-packed with meetings and my inbox seemed to grow exponentially since the last time I'd checked. Which reminded me it was time to fill the vacant admin role.

"Well?" she asked.

I met her waiting gaze. "No."

*Three.*

*Two.*

*One.*

"I know you didn't just tell me no," she snapped.

Never failed. My sister was the oldest of the group. By the time I was born, she was already married with a kid. Since Momma worked, Sabrina served as a stand-in mother. At one point, she'd even offered to raise me herself, but my parents weren't playing that shit. That didn't stop her from trying to dictate my life.

"I did," I told her, leaning back in my chair. "My answer hasn't changed since last year. I have too much on my plate with work."

"You own this company," she argued. "You can take time for what's important."

I tapped my pen on the desk. "My work is important. To me."

"Baby brother, it's one event," she insisted. "A couple of hours out of your day. Besides, I thought it would be a great opportunity for you to meet one of our board members."

*I should've known there was more to the story.*

"She's a lovely woman, successful. She's divorced and—"

"Hell no." The last time my sister tried to hook me up, I ended up at the restaurant of the woman's ex-husband who wanted her back. After I almost dragged that man in front of his patrons and employees, I vowed to never go out with someone Sabrina thought was 'lovely'.

"Spencer Lavell Cross."

"Sabrina, stop," I warned. "If you need cash, I got you. But my time isn't up for negotiation—not for your event or for your board member."

I turned my attention back to my computer. As I scrolled, an unread message from Alaiya caught my eye.

*To: Spencer Cross*
*From: Alaiya Young*
*Subject: Urgent*

Realtor got back to me this morning on the Martz property. Potential offer on the table. Meet me there at 1:00 pm.

Best,
Alaiya

Glancing at my watch, I grumbled a curse. It was already past noon. I closed my laptop and stood.

"Wait?" Sabrina called. "Where are you going?"

I kissed her brow. "Sis, it is the middle of the workday. I have shit to do. Send me the sponsorship forms and I'll see what I can do."

TWENTY MINUTES LATER, I approached the entrance to the building where Alaiya was standing. "Is it too late?"

She smiled, shaking her head. "You're good. Did you get a chance to review the numbers?" After years of working with Alaiya, we were a well-oiled machine. Our history was an added benefit because she knew when to push and when to pull back. "The seller is willing to take less than offering if you complete the build."

Over the past several years, an influx of home builders had bought up empty lots in the area. New houses were sprouting up like weeds. In this case, the builder halted construction on two lots for personal reasons and needed to sell quickly. As with every property I considered, I took a moment to assess the condition of the structures.

"When does he need to know?" I asked, finally stepping into the first house.

"This afternoon," she said.

"Do you have any experience with him?"

"Yes." She walked around the front room, brushed her hand over the unfinished countertop in the kitchen. "I worked with him on a deal last year."

"Why is he selling?"

"I don't know for sure, but rumor has it he's in some financial trouble. A lot of debt. Too many commitments. He wants the property to go to someone who gives a shit about the community."

I glanced at her. "Is he from the area?"

"His wife grew up in Ann Arbor. They settled here after they got married, raised their kids, then moved toward Detroit. But he wanted to rebuild her grandmother's old neighborhood."

"Good plan," I murmured, peering up at the exposed beams on the ceiling.

"What do you think?" I couldn't help but smile when she rubbed her glove-covered hands together. "It's cold as hell in here."

I met her waiting gaze. It had been a couple of weeks since the Mistletoe Match and we'd communicated via email and text, but I hadn't seen her in person since then. "What do you think?"

Pulling her coat closed, she scanned the space. "I love it. Lots of light. Perfect size for one person, but still cozy enough for a small family. What is your end game?"

Initially, I thought about flipping it and selling to one of my tenants looking to buy. But Laiya brought up a valid point. "Would you move here?"

She smiled. "I've never really cared for new builds, but it's quaint. Great location. Private." She nibbled on her bottom lip. "I probably would. Why?"

"Just thinking … Weighing my options."

"I could see myself enjoying the process of making it my own. If you decide to purchase, maybe you can have your tenants choose their own fixtures, paint, landscaping … Bring them in on the project. They'd like that."

Seeing the way her face lit up when she talked about this house made my decision easier. "Draw up an offer, contingent on my ability to finish the build at a reasonable cost."

She pulled out her tablet, set it up on the countertop, and started typing. "Who are you thinking about for the construction?"

"What about your guy?"

"Preston?" she asked.

"Is that your cousin's husband?"

"Yeah. I'm supposed to see them New Year's Day. Better yet …" She pulled out her phone and made a call.

Soon we were on the line with Preston Hayes. While I talked to him about the project, she forwarded pictures of both homes. Since it was freezing, we took the conversation to her car, and by the time we finished discussing the particulars, I was confident I'd be able to take it on.

As she worked on the purchase agreement, I stared at her. "How are you?"

She froze, glancing at me out of the corner of her eye. "I'm fine."

"Laiya, how are you?" I repeated.

Letting out a heavy sigh, she confessed, "No, really. I'm good. Rod had a change of heart and returned the money. He told me it was because he loved me, but I knew Des lit him up after he drained the accounts. And he doesn't want to lose her. We decided to do an uncontested divorce and he moved out a couple of days ago." She snickered. "Left all his shit, though. Told me to deal with it. And I haven't heard from him since."

The more she told me about Rod, the more I wanted to whoop his ass. My jaw clenched as irrational rage coated my insides. *Irrational* because … Again, none of this was my business. Laiya was a grown-ass woman capable of taking care of herself. Still didn't stop me from wanted to fight this battle for her.

"What do you need?"

"Nothing," she said with a shrug. "My attorney prepared the settlement agreement, filed it with the court. Our date is set." She looked at me. "A huge weight has been lifted."

"But …"

"No buts. It's so over and I'm okay with that."

We settled into a comfortable silence as she finished the purchase offer. Once she was done, she let me read it, made a few changes, and finally hit SEND.

"That's it. Just waiting to hear back."

I pulled out my phone and scrolled through my email. "You have any plans today?"

She slipped me a curious glance. "Other than work?"

"Yeah."

"No, I'll be at home surrounded by all the things I need to get rid of."

I chuckled, pulling out a bag and handing it to her.

"What's this?" she asked.

I leaned closer. "Gummies."

Her eyes lit up as she gaped. "You brought me weed?"

Unable to help myself, I barked out a laugh. When I picked up my supply for The Leaf Lodge, I'd grabbed a low-dose bag for her. Figured I'd help her out on her list when the time was right. "You said you wanted to try an edible, so I got you some."

"Oh." She studied the bag. "Is it strong?"

"It can be, if you eat the whole bag."

"Okay." She nibbled on her thumbnail. "I'm gonna try it."

"Start with half of one. If you feel okay, then take the other half."

With a hard nod, she stuffed the bag in her purse. "Got it."

Before I could warn her about side effects, she hugged me. And I … *Damn*, I wanted to take up residence inside of her. She felt so warm, so good against me that I didn't want to let her go.

Unfortunately, she pulled away from me. Clearing her throat, she tucked a strand a hair behind her ear. "Um, that was … I didn't mean to do that."

"Don't apologize," I assured her. "I liked it."

She groaned. "Well, then. Um. I should probably get to the office. I have some work to catch up on."

I could take the hint, so I changed the subject. "While I have you here, though, I've put together a list of objectives for the new year. Number one on the list is commercial space. Taylar is looking for an event venue, and I told her I would invest."

Alaiya placed a hand over her heart. "Aw, I love it. You're such a good uncle. Lease or purchase?"

"I'm open."

"Sounds good."

I slid on my skull cap and opened the door. "Take it easy, Laiya."

She gripped the steering wheel. "Bye, Spence. And thank you."

———

*Alaiya*

I CAN'T FEEL *my face*.

I froze at the self-checkout lane at Sam's Club and glanced at the various people standing around. Lifting my hands to my face, I pinched my nose, brushed my palm over my eyes, and tugged on my ears. Everything was there. But not there. And that didn't make any sense.

"Mom?" Desiree shoved me gently. "It's our turn."

I blinked once. Then another time for good measure. When it felt like my legs were going to give out, I gripped the cart for dear life. "Oh shit," I mumbled.

Des glanced at me over her shoulder. "What's wrong?"

"I feel weird."

Walking over to me, Des peered at me. "What do you mean?"

"I'm probably having a stroke."

Alarmed, Des' mouth fell open. "Mom, don't play."

I ran a finger down her face. Her skin was so soft. I remembered having skin like that … fifty million years ago. I held her cheeks in my palms. "You're so cute. My little Mucha Mucha."

Des gasped. "Oh God. What's wrong with you?"

Holding my hand up, I studied my ashy knuckles. "I forgot my hand lotion."

She squeezed my shoulders. "Focus, Mom." Des paid for our cart and escorted me out of the store. "I should call someone. Shit, I can't call Dad. Aunt Vicki?"

The moment the name registered in my brain, I yelled, "No!" I smacked my hand over my mouth. "Shh."

"Mom, you're telling me to shh, but you're the one yelling in the parking lot."

"Don't call her," I whisper-yelled.

"Well, then we're going to the hospital," Des said, helping me into the car. "I don't know what else to do."

"Des, is my nose on my face?" I smacked my cheek to make sure. "'Cause I think I left it in the store."

"What? Wait, what did you eat today?"

"I don't know." I gasped. "Oh no! I didn't eat." My throat burned as tears welled up in my eyes. "I'm starving and having a stroke."

"Oh Lord," Des muttered. "Listen to me, Mom. Did you drink that smoothie in the refrigerator?"

"Smoothie?"

"Yes, the green one."

"I don't know what you're talking about," I mumbled, burrowing into the seat. "I'm so sleepy. If I die, make sure you don't show anyone my panties. I had to put on an old pair this morning. Oh, and ignore my browsing history. I just wanted to see Drake's dick because it was all on the internet. And I was rushing so I didn't notice they had a hole in them."

Des giggled. "Mom, you're trippin'. Everybody saw that video. You'll be fine."

"Don't tell anyone, but I haven't seen a physical dick in months."

"Stop," she ordered. "I love that you're talking to me, but can we draw the line at male parts? Think back and tell me if you tasted the popcorn in that little baggie in the pantry. What about a piece of candy?"

"That's it!" I clapped. "Spencer gave me gummies."

"Mr. Spencer?" Des asked. "As in Spencer Cross?"

"Yeah." I smiled. "With his fine self."

"We're getting somewhere. What kind of gummy?"

I glanced over at her. At twenty-four years old, she was a rockstar. Talented. Intelligent. Gifted. Perfect. "I'm so proud of you, babe. You're amazing."

"Thanks, Mom. I need you to calm down, though. It's the edible."

"What?" Panic welled inside. "I had an edible?"

"You just said you ate a gummy."

"Oh." My shoulders fell. "Right. I had one."

"Just one?" she asked.

"Or two."

"Two?" She pulled over in McDonald's parking lot. "And you didn't eat anything?"

"Nope. Just a piece of cheese. And a grape."

"Who eats just one grape?"

"Your mother." I shrugged. "I was busy."

Des massaged her temples. "Maybe you should eat something with substance." She pulled into the drive-thru and ordered a small fry and three bottles of water. "This should help."

I ate a few fries in the car, then guzzled down one bottle of water. "I'm full."

"Try to drink more," she pressed. "You need to stay hydrated."

"I'm sleepy."

"Okay, I have to run into Marshall's really quick. I need one more Christmas gift."

I perked up. "Good. I love shopping."

She turned the car off and glanced at me. "I don't want to leave you alone in the car. Are you feeling a little steadier now?"

Waving a dismissive hand her way, I assured her, "I'll be fine."

When we entered the store, I nearly tripped over the wheel of a cart. Des steadied me with her hand. "This was a mistake. Let's go."

"No." I swatted her hand away and ventured toward the shoe section. "I'm fine." *Except…*

I couldn't concentrate. And my feet were huge. I was a giant and my footsteps were loud as hell. And my head was probably as big as the people in Sam's Club. I stopped in my tracks, turning to Des. "I have to sit down."

"Lord, why is this my life?" Des looped her arm through mine and led me back toward the door. She helped me get in the car again. "I'm taking you home."

A loud ring boomed over the speaker. I screamed. And Des shushed me.

"Hello?" she said.

Spence's voice came over the speaker. "What's up, Des?"

"You gave my mother an edible, and I just want to let the record show that you fucked up."

His soft chuckle made me smile. "He even laughs sexy," I murmured.

"What?" Spence said.

"Huh?" Des muttered a curse and handed me a bottle of water. "Drink this and be quiet."

I tried to pull the top off, but it wouldn't budge. Shaking the bottle, I complained, "This isn't working."

"Mr. Spence, we're fine but I thought you should know."

"Where are you?" he asked.

I giggled. "Waiting for you."

"Anyway," Des cut in, "you owe me."

"Let me know if you need anything," he said. "Get some sleep, Laiya."

"I am sleepy," I told him. "So sleepy. And hungry. And sad. And happy. And floating."

"See what you did," Des announced. "This is a hot mess. I gotta go."

Once we made it home, Des helped me inside, just in time for my legs to give out. I crawled to the family room.

She tried to help me up. "Hold on, mom. Let me—"

"I'm fine. Just need to go to sleep."

After pulling myself up on the couch, I rolled on my back. The room was spinning, my nose was still gone, but my ears worked just fine because I heard everything. Des' footsteps echoed in the hallway, her voice piercing my ears as she talked to someone on the phone. The ice machine clanged in my brain and the television volume was too high to focus.

"Turn it off," I grumbled.

Des placed a blanket over me. "Sleep, Mom. When you wake up, everything will be okay."

"Stop yelling at me."

She laughed. "I'm not yelling, but okay. I'll leave you alone. Check on you in a bit."

My eyes fluttered closed, then there was nothing.


I JUMPED UP WITH A START, frantically looking around at my surroundings. Frowning, I glanced at my watch. *Six o'clock*? It was just noon. I'd lost six hours. "Oh my God," I whispered. "My head is heavy."

"You probably need to sleep more."

The low, very male, very raspy voice caught me off guard and I yelped, sliding off the couch onto the floor. I spun toward the sound. "What are you doing here?"

Spence crossed the room to me, held out his hand, and helped me up. "I stopped by to check on you."

I tugged on my bunched-up shirt. "This is your fault."

He laughed softly. "I'll take full responsibility."

Sitting down on the couch again, I spotted a full glass of water. "Is this mine?"

"Yeah."

"Where's Des?" I gulped the water.

"She went to dinner with her friends. I told her I'd stay with you until you woke up … or she got home. Whichever happened first."

I groaned. "I'm so embarrassed. I can't believe I acted like a lunatic in public."

"You remember?"

My mind turned over the hazy details. There were some blind spots in my memory, but not enough to make me feel better about my behavior. "What did she tell you?"

He hunched a shoulder. "Everything from Sam's Club to

McDonald's to Marshalls. If it makes you feel better, she was very amused."

"It doesn't." I blew out a slow breath. "I don't know why I didn't listen to you."

"How much did you eat?"

"One. Maybe two. I'll tell you one thing, though … Never afuckingain."

Spence sat down next to me, bumped my shoulder with his. "I'm sorry. At least you were able to cross something off of your list."

I rolled my eyes. *That shit hurts*. Massaging my temple, I said, "Forget that damn list."

"Sure about that?"

I shot him a sidelong glance. "Maybe. Why?"

He walked to the door. "'Cause I got you something."

"What did you get me?" When he didn't answer, I shuffled over to the window. Frowning, I peered through the blinds and gasped. "You got me a dumpster?"

His mouth curved into a sexy half-smile, half-smirk. "For the purge."

I stared at him in disbelief, holding my hands to my mouth as the reality of his gesture sunk in. He'd bought me something so practical, so thoughtful, so on-time. That dumpster was better than any bouquet of flowers, every high-priced dinner at a swanky restaurant, and all the gifts I'd ever received. Because it meant he'd listened to me, he'd considered my feelings. And I wanted to cry. I wanted to laugh. I wanted to melt into his arms. But I wouldn't.

"Thank you," I whispered, fighting the fresh tears that welled up in my eyes.

"You don't have to thank me."

"No," I shook my head, "I do."

We stared at each other for a moment, while I struggled to hold it together.

"I can't believe you did this for me. Thank you so much."

He cupped my face in his massive hand, brushing my jawline with his thumb. "Anything you need. Told you I got you."

I bit down on my bottom lip. "I appreciate you. Now I just have to figure out what to move first." A wave a dizziness swept over me, and I leaned against the wall. "And if I can even stand up straight much longer. I'm definitely still high."

Spence cracked up. "Sit yo' ass down."

He walked me over to the couch and helped me get situated.

Once I was seated, glass of water full, blanket over my legs, he said, "You got me for a few hours. Just tell me where to start."

My heart pounded in my ears as I peered up at him. In an instant, I was transported back to that playground. Riding the Merry-Go-Round as he watched me eat that sandwich. It was a simple gesture, but it was also a lifeline. One that had never been severed despite our choices.

"Why are you here?" I whispered. "Why are you like this?"

A soft smile formed on his perfect lips. He bent down, meeting my gaze. "I could ask you the same thing."

"I'm at home. But you're here. And you don't have to be here. Why?"

"I told you …" He shrugged. "I can't walk away."

"What does this mean?"

Spence searched my eyes. "It means what I said."

Reaching out to him, I brushed my fingers over his chiseled jaw. "I'm still married."

"You are."

"If you keep doing this, I might not be able to run away from you."

"Is that what you did then?"

The air changed around us and everything in the room— the Christmas tree in the corner, the lamp on the table, the television in the background—faded away. In the past, I would've changed the subject, pulled away, closed off the part of myself that always felt too much whenever he was around.

"I can't tell you," I whispered.

"You can tell me anything."

I shook my head. "If I do, then the last twenty-five years didn't mean anything, and I know it did."

He held my hand against his face, placed a soft kiss to my palm. "Two things can be true at the same time. But … you can also have a regret so big that it takes up all the empty space in your mind."

"Is that how you feel?"

"Are you ready to hear how I feel?"

"Spence," I bit down on my bottom lip, "you told me that you wanted me."

"I do," he confirmed. "I also want *this*. The conversations. The silent understanding. The jokes. The work."

"Can we have all of that?"

"We have it now." He rested his forehead against mine. My body ached with the need to touch him. To *be* touched. Tingles flitted across my skin, from the tips of my fingers to my toes. He hadn't even kissed me yet, but it felt like he did. "But we can have more."

*I want more.*

I loved Rod, I'd built a life with him. I still cared for him. But …

*I love Spence, too.* How could that be true? How could I have spent years with one man and still feel so much for another? "I still can't say it."

Spence kissed my brow. "You don't have to. I already know. I told you what I wanted. When you're ready, I'll be waiting." He stood. "Until then, this doesn't change anything. I'm here for you. Always." He scanned the room. "Now, what should I throw out first?"

Smiling, I looked at that ugly-ass clock on the end table, the one Rod's mother bought us for our wedding. "Throw that shit away."

"I got you."

For the next several hours, I pointed out the things I didn't want anymore, and Spence *purged*. Something happened at the Mistletoe Match that had changed the game for us, opened a door that I once thought was closed forever. Yet, the questions remained … *Am I ready? Can I cross the line?*

I still wasn't sure where this would lead. Spence was a man of his word, *the* man I could always count on. He was my colleague, my friend. *Can he be my lover? Can I let him?* The emotional distance between us hadn't changed the underlying need to be there for each other. Even if it was a simple save at a dating event or a thoughtful gift during a rough time. I knew I could call him if I needed him. He would never make crazy demands for my time or energy. He'd never hold what he did for me over my head. He wouldn't expect anything in return. And for the first time in a long time, I felt safe. I felt hope. *I feel free.*

# CHAPTER 4

## You're All I Need to Get By

*Spencer*

*Two Months Later*

Every Sunday, my mother used to drag us to church. It wasn't one of those huge mega churches, either. It was a small, white church surrounded by an open field. Almost picturesque except it was surrounded by one of the worst hoods in the city. Crime was rampant, cars were stolen out of the parking lot across the street, unkempt addicts sometimes barged in the sanctuary during service, but inside was like a bubble of congregational songs and long prayers.

Most of the members were women. Older women with peppermints in their purses, doilies on their laps, and tambourines in their palms. We'd would sit there for hours, first through Sunday school, then praise and worship, followed by testimony service, and finally the sermon. Communion Sundays made the days even longer, but at least we had fellowship dinner afterward. To this day, there was nothing like Pastor Minor's fried chicken or Mother Pearl's salty green beans with ham hocks. Generally, I remembered that time fondly, especially the lessons learned like Father Abraham having many sons, God specializing in things that seem impossible, and most importantly, God is the Solid Rock on which to stand.

The bubble of acceptance within the congregation busted sometime around eleventh grade. That's when I discovered sex and bud. At that point, I was labeled a bad influence. Whenever I walked into the temple, the same women who'd hugged me every Sunday glared at me. The pastor called me up to the altar to pray the rebellion away. And Mama ... well, she told every last one of them people off.

I still remembered the conversation she had with me on the way home, the look she had in her eyes, the love in her voice.

*Son, I know you'll do the right thing. Just remember God sees everything and He loves you.*

While Mama continued to put God first, I never returned to that church. My mother never brought it up again, but she supported me when I purchased my first home, when I started Cross Investments, and even when I told her I wanted to dip my feet into the cannabis industry. A couple of years ago, she died after a long, drawn-out battle with cancer. Because of her Christian belief, she'd suffered excruciating pain, sometimes crying herself to sleep. Until I convinced her to try a cannabis smoothie.

When Michigan legalized weed, I incorporated it into my business. Opening The Leaf Lodge allowed me the opportunity to help people like her. Of course, we rented to travelers looking for different types of experiences. But we also hosted several retreats for women and men who struggled with debilitating physical or mental illnesses, people who just needed space to convalesce. I wanted to take the stigma out of using the substance for medicinal purposes while celebrating the strides we'd made in the industry. And days like today strengthened my resolve to expand.

"So," Des nibbled on her thumb, "what do you think?"

I finished off the acai bowl. "Mmm hmm." I nodded, popping the last blueberry in my mouth. "It's good."

She rested her elbows on the table, a tentative grin on her face. "Can you taste it?"

"Not at all," I confirmed.

"Figured it would be a refreshing treat at the retreat next weekend," she explained. "It's easy to make, and we can keep several in the fridge in case guests want a snack."

I gave her a fist bump. "Great idea."

"I used sativa, but an indica strain would work as well. In case they want to eat at night."

When I started Cross Investments, I entered the business world with my head in the clouds. I dreamed of the portfolio, the money, the connections. I believed my own hype, so I started too many projects, made some promises I couldn't keep, bruised relationships with contractors, and missed important deadlines. The work that had once excited me ended up suffocating me. And I failed spectacularly.

To survive after the first year, I had to shift my priorities, manage my own expectations. I wrote down three goals for my second year—continuing education, dream team, growth. In that order. I already had a degree in finance, so I under-stood cash flow, but I lacked fundamental knowledge in every other area that mattered. Instead of moving forward, I paused all acquisitions and started at one. I enrolled in several classes from property management to construction basics, earned a real estate appraisal license. I also took the Michigan Real Estate agent prelicensure course and worked as a Realtor for a year. Then, I poured my resources into one area—single-family rental housing. It wasn't until I'd been in business for myself for years that I expanded to short-term rentals and vacation homes.

My team—Des included—was on their shit.

"You might even try a hybrid," I suggested, tossing the empty bowl into the trashcan next to the sliding glass door.

Des scribbled a note. Advances in technology made keeping notes easier, but she was like me in that she always carried a physical planner with her. "I'll try it tomorrow." She slid a piece of paper over to me. "I've also finalized the itinerary. Bianca confirmed this morning."

I scanned the document. "Did she send an invoice?"

Bianca Warren was a registered nurse, with a specialty in the therapeutic use of cannabis for symptom management. She'd been an invaluable consultant for my business and always made herself available to our guests before, during, and after our wellness retreats.

"In your inbox. I copied you on my request to accounts payable."

"Perfect."

Des opened her tablet.

"Anything else I should know?" I asked.

Des blew out a slow breath. "Yeah." She bit down on her stylus. "Some of my friends from college are coming to town for March Madness. I was wondering if we could use the Triple B." She smiled. "Of course, they'd pay. Or I would."

Frowning, I asked, "What is a Triple B?"

She shrugged. "Oh, it's what I've been calling The Leaf Lodge. Bud, Bed, and Breakfast."

A smile tugged at my lips. "I think I like that," I confessed.

Des taught me something different in every conversation. In college, she'd majored in environmental science, but she was well read and knew something about everything from plant biology to marketing to sustainability. Since she started working for me, we increased our social media engagement, improved the energy efficiency in our properties, and reduced waste by implementing recycling and composting programs.

"Let's use it in the next IG and TikTok campaign."

She jotted a note. "You know I got you."

I knew Des wanted to do more than work for me, but I selfishly hoped she'd stick around a little longer. I had to fight the urge to throw more money at her because I didn't want to tempt her to stay if her heart was pulling her elsewhere. "And you don't have to pay to stay here."

Her eyes snapped to mine. "What?"

"Consider it a perk of your employment. And payback for giving your mother that edible."

"Thanks." She walked around the bar and gave me a hug. "My friends are going to be so excited."

The front door opened behind me, and I turned in time to see Alaiya step inside. When she spotted us, she smiled. "Hey. Hope I didn't get here too early. I know you two had a one-on-one."

"Mom." Des rushed over to her mother, giving her a hug. "Mr. Spencer is going to let us stay here next month."

Laiya's gaze locked on mine. "That's good. I don't have to disappear in my bedroom now." She walked toward the table, dropped her bag on the sofa, and took a seat. "Thanks for saving me."

I sipped my coffee. "Always."

Clearing her throat, she announced, "Allow me to make your day, Spence."

I gave her a sidelong glance. "What's up?"

"The seller accepted your offer on the Pineview building."

Des grinned. "That's great. Isn't that the one Taylar was eyeing for her event venue?"

I held up my hand, and Alaiya gave me a high-five.

"Yes," I answered. "She'll be happy to hear that."

"I think it's awesome you're helping her with this," Des mused.

"She's putting up most of the capital. I just helped a little bit."

"A lot," Alaiya corrected. "But you rarely take the credit."

I hunched a shoulder. "It's not mine to take. It was a group effort, and this deal helps us all. A building for Taylar, an investment opportunity for me," my eyes connected with hers again, "and a hefty commission for you."

"He's right, Mom," Des agreed. "This is a win for AY Realty."

"More money? No problem," I teased, calling back to the number-one item on her checklist.

Alaiya averted her gaze, obviously catching the reference. "What's this?" She grabbed an acai bowl, changing the topic. "Looks delicious."

"Wait," Des shouted.

Pulling the bowl away from Laiya, I warned, "That's probably not a good idea."

Laiya snatched it back. "I don't like it when people tell me what to do."

"I didn't just meet you yesterday. I know you. And *this*," I slid the bowl back to Des, "is not for you."

"Mom, it has weed in it," Des explained.

Laiya's mouth snapped shut. "Oh." She pouted. "Okay."

"But I can make you one. Shouldn't take more than ten minutes. Be right back." Des disappeared into the kitchen, leaving me alone with Laiya.

And her scent.

And her lips.

And that body.

My composure was dangling on a very precarious string. Two months ago, I almost kissed her. But I wanted to be respectful of her situation. Now I couldn't think of a good enough reason not to finish what I'd started that night. It seemed I was in a constant state of denial about my ability to maintain control of my emotions when I was around her.

We'd reverted back to business as usual, despite everything we'd shared in December. It was torture, seeing her around, pretending I didn't want her. And I tried—*I really did*—to be okay with it. But …

*I'm not.*

I couldn't go back to a time before I made my intentions clear, before I'd promised to give her everything she needed to move the fuck on. I hadn't planned on laying my cards on the table, but I couldn't stop myself either. Although I told her I'd wait until she was officially single, I wanted to set her free now. For me. *Only me.*

I reached over, wrapped my hand around her wrist, and brought it up to my mouth, rubbing her skin with my nose. "You smell good," I confessed.

"Spence," she whispered, "you can't do this."

"Like pears and vanilla," I murmured, darting my tongue out to lick her.

A burst of air escaped her lips, and I wanted to swallow it. I wanted to taste her, to bury my face in her pussy, to hear her groan my name. Mostly, I wanted to consume her, to brand her. Like she'd done to me that day on the playground, before I knew what to do with it, how to handle it.

I traced the lines of the small tattoo on her wrist with my tongue. "Are you divorced yet?"

"Oh God," she muttered. "Oh shit. No."

"When?"

"I can't think, Spence."

"Just reaffirming my intention to make you mine," I admitted softly.

"What makes you think I want to be yours?"

Without warning, I gripped the arm of the chair and pulled her closer to me.

She yelped. "Spence?" She glanced at the door to the kitchen, but when she met my eyes again, there was delight in them, not trepidation. "What are you doing?"

"We need to have a talk," I told her.

"What? I ..." She sighed. "Okay, talk."

"I'm too old to not be real."

The corners of her mouth quirked up. "Even when you were young, you were real."

"I'm glad you know that." I picked up her hand again, bringing it to my lips and placing a kiss to her palm. "You also know how I feel about my time." A surefire way to piss me off? Waste my damn time.

"I do," she said.

"I wouldn't say this is a fault, but I take people at their word. One of my biggest regrets? Letting you marry that clown-ass nigga."

She gaped at me. "Spencer!"

I loved the way she said my name. "Alaiya."

"I was convinced I was doing the right thing."

"And I took you at your word. I married Jasmine for the same reason. But here we are. Nothing and no one standing between us. If we can make this work, I don't want to waste any more time."

Neither of us spoke for a moment. The air between us was thick with a tension that was once unspoken but always there. Before I had to ignore it. Because she wasn't mine to have. Now, *we* could choose to give into it.

"I need time to think about this," she said.

Swallowing hard, I lowered my head as heaviness settled over my body. Because I'd never push her. I wouldn't make her feel like she had to choose me. No matter how much I wanted her to. "Okay."

"Spence?"

Glancing up at her, I forced myself to smile. "Yes."

Then, her lips were on mine, shocking the hell out of me. She pulled back before I was ready to let her go. Smiling, she said, "I thought about it."

I laughed. "That fast, huh?"

"I've been thinking about it since the playground."

Pulling her to me, I brushed my lips over hers again. Then, once more before deepening the kiss.

*Damn*. Everything about her was perfect, everything about us was right—her fingertips against my jaw, the feel of her nose bumping mine, the way she groaned when I dipped my tongue inside of her mouth.

"Oh. My. God!"

Des' voice broke through the fog, and Alaiya jumped back so hard her chair tipped over and she toppled to the floor. Jumping into action, I helped her up. It took us a moment to get ourselves together, but once Laiya was on her feet, we turned to face Des.

"Mom!" Des screeched, her gaze flitting from me to her mother rapidly. She squeezed her eyes shut and when she opened them again, they connected with mine. "Mr. Spencer! You kissed my mother."

Alaiya stepped forward. "Technically, I kissed him first."

I scratched my temple. "But it was a mutual thing."

"How long has this been going on?" Des asked.

"Today."

"Forever."

Our simultaneous responses kind of drowned each other out, but I glanced at her. "Really, Laiya? Today?"

She shrugged. "Yes."

"What she means is today is the first time we acted on it," I explained.

"*Ever*," Laiya reiterated. She rubbed Des' shoulders. "We've known each other for a long time, you know that. And ..." She looked at me, eyes wide. "Spence, please?" She mouthed, "help me."

Taking her cue, I pulled out a chair. "Have a seat, Des."

Des seemed to consider the offer to talk, but she didn't move. "I don't need to sit," she said. "And you don't need to explain yourselves. I just need to drink a bottle of wine, take a nap, and start over."

"Babe," Laiya said.

Des held up a hand. "No. No, Mom. I just need a time out." She turned to me. "I'm gonna go. I'll email you the final menu later."

I nodded. "It can wait 'til the morning."

A few minutes later, Des was gone. When Laiya plopped in an empty chair, I asked, "Are you okay?"

"I was careless. I should've never done that."

I knelt down on one knee in front of her. "It's not your fault."

"Spence, we traumatized my daughter." Tears filled her eyes. I hated to see her cry. "Des is a grown woman, but she's still Rod's daughter. She loves her father. I have to make sure she's good with this before we …"

The rest of the sentence hung in the air. Des wasn't *just* Alaiya's daughter. She was a huge part of my business, my life. "I get it."

"Next Friday," she blurted out.

I blinked, confused about the change in subject. "What?"

"That's when the divorce is final." Laiya flashed a wobbly smile. "Figured you'd want to know."

"I did want to know."

She stood. "I should probably go."

I walked her to the door. "If you need me …"

She gripped my shirt in her fist, stepped up on her toes, and kissed me. "I'll call you."

# CHAPTER 5

## *So High*

*Alaiya*

"What the fuck do you have on?"

I froze, my mouth wide open. "Wh—" I looked down, only to make sure my pants weren't inside out or my shoes mismatched. "What are you talking about?"

"Laiya!" My cousin Dallas stalked over to me, circling me. "I love you, cuzzie, but you're not going out with me looking like Florida Evans at James' funeral."

My little cousin, Blake, snorted, spitting out the water she'd just gulped down. "Damn. Damn. Damn."

The room erupted with laughter as they broke out in a silly rendition of the *Good Times* theme song. I glared at all of my cousins—Blake, Bliss, Dallas, and Demi. "I should kick all y'all heffas out."

Bliss walked over to me. "I'm sorry, Laiya." She was my

nice, sweet cousin. Full of cheer and love and encouragement. "But they're right."

My tentative smile fell. "Traitor."

Bliss giggled. "It's a party."

"You look like work," Blake added.

"No," Dallas chimed in again, "she looks like she's in mourning. All that grey."

"That outfit is not it," Demi said. "Especially since you just got the best news in court today." The divorce was finalized, the judgment signed, and I was officially single. And because Demi was *the* best attorney, it was mostly painless.

The process was nothing like the movies. There were no courtroom outbursts, no veiled threats, no crazy drama. Just two people who had finally accepted that the marriage was over. And although Rod and I couldn't make it work, I hoped that we could one day become friends again.

"I know." My throat burned as fresh tears fell. "I can't thank you enough."

Bliss smoothed a comforting hand over my back. "Don't cry, cuzzie."

I wiped my face with the back of my hand. "I've been crying all day."

"I know you're not having second thoughts," Blake said. "Not after everything you've been through."

Each of my cousins had a little bit of Aunt Vicki in them. Dallas was bossy. She fixed shit for everyone. Blake was never scared to fight. Bliss' heart was big, and she loved hard. And Demi—even though she wasn't Aunt Vicki's biological daughter—had picked up my aunt's ability to read a room.

Growing up, I didn't have a lot of friends. But finding Aunt Vicki had opened up a world of true friendship in the form of my cousins. They were younger, but wise beyond their years. And I was blessed to have them in my life.

Another tear escaped. "I don't have any regrets about the divorce, Blake."

"Good because I was about to say …"

"Be quiet, Sissy," Bliss ordered her twin. "You're not at work, and Laiya is not your client. She ended the relationship. Now, it's up to me." While they were both relationship experts, Blake helped women break up with their significant others and Bliss was the matchmaker. "When you're ready to date again, call me."

Dallas rolled her eyes. "In the meantime, no one died and—"

"Technically, her relationship died," Demi argued.

"Again, no one died." Dallas tugged at my dress. "Is this wool?"

"Cashmere," I corrected.

"Can you say hot as hell?" Blake fanned herself. "Shit, just looking at you is making me sweat."

"Girl, you're pregnant," Demi mused.

My mouth fell open. "Blake, are you having a baby?"

Blake glared at me. "That would be a hell nah. My vagina is not ready to have a big head baby. Right now, it's enjoying Lennox's dick."

I shoved her away playfully. "You're so stupid."

"Anyway," Bliss shook her head at her sister, "don't listen to her. She'll be pregnant before the year is out."

"In your dreams," Blake muttered. "If anyone is going to be pregnant by the end of the year, it's going to be Demi's ass."

I spun around to face Demi. "Are you and Duke trying? Why do I feel like I'm so out of the loop?"

Demi fell in love with my Aunt Vicki's son, Duke. Which came as a surprise to no one except them.

"We know how to make sure that doesn't happen," Demi assured.

Dallas scoffed. "You just had a scare last month."

Demi thumped Dallas on her ear.

"Ouch." Dallas frowned. "That shit hurt."

"Don't tell my business," Demi grumbled through clenched teeth. "'Cause I can tell yours."

"But we won't do that." Dallas plastered a grin on her face. "Today is about Laiya."

"No, it's about Sloan and Maddox," I insisted. "We're celebrating their pending nuptials, not my divorce.

My cousin, Sloane, had shocked the hell out of all of us when she finally agreed to marry the love of her life, Maddox. The two had been dating for a while, but she'd been adamant that marriage wasn't in their cards. Until it was. Even more surprising was the fact that they were doing everything the traditional way. Engagement party, bridal shower, bridal luncheon, rehearsal dinner, welcome party, and everything else that went with it.

Walking over to the mirror, I assessed my appearance. As much as I hated to admit it, they were right. This wasn't a somber occasion, it was an engagement party. And I'd bathed in grey. The sweater dress worked for the office, for when I was showing houses, or …

*A memorial service.*

My hair … yeah, the sleek ponytail would work for the club or …

*A funeral.*

And the knee-length tweed coat I bought would've paired well at a church convention or …

*A burial site.*

"Are they really going to put us through months of this shit?" Blake asked, studying her nails. "These wedding events are too much."

"Of course it's too much for you, Sissy," Bliss agreed. "You dipped out of your own wedding to elope."

"And did," Blake said. "I'd do that shit again, too. Bottom line … I married. I'm happy. And I'm not pregnant."

I giggled. "You're silly, Blake. But I will say, I think Sloan is doing this for Uncle Linc."

Bliss sipped her wine. "No, she's doing it for herself. She's so in love that she wants a redo since her first husband demanded a Christmas wedding. She wants good weather, no snow, and all of her friends and family in attendance."

"Good for her," I said.

"Okay, that's enough talking. I need you to get yourself together, Laiya," Dallas ordered, pointing toward my bedroom. "I'm giving you one more chance to come out looking stunning. If you fail the next test, I'm delving into your closet myself."

Without a word, I turned around and walked back into my room. The last couple of months had been a nightmare. Between court dates, attempted mediation, work, and arguments with Rod about the house, I was exhausted. Tonight was an opportunity to let my hair down, to celebrate my cousin's engagement with family and friends.

After a few minutes, I'd given up on 'stunning' and went for comfortable, pulling out my signature all-black. Since it was still cold as hell and snowing, I chose a long-sleeved jumpsuit with an off-the-shoulder ruffle. I planned to wear black boots.

When I emerged from my room, Des had joined them. "Hey, babe. You're here."

Although we lived in the same house, Des had pretty much been absent the last couple of weeks. We'd always been close. She was my road dog, my favorite person in the world. I didn't want this potential thing with Spence to impact my relationship with my daughter. I needed her to be good with this before I could be good with it. She'd assured me she wasn't upset, but I was worried. Especially since I would see Spence tonight. After all, he was Maddox's uncle.

"Just left Dad," Des told me. "I wanted to check in on him."

Des had chosen not to come to the courthouse today, and I didn't blame her. "How is he?" I asked.

"He's good." She approached me, wrapped her arms around me, and hugged me. "I'm sorry, Mom," she whispered. "I've been bitchy, and you don't deserve that."

I brushed a hand over her cheek. "You're fine, babe."

She shook her head. "No, I'm not a child but I acted like one."

"You're *my* child. You matter to me."

"When you told me you were filing for divorce, I was glad. Dad snores, but that wasn't the reason he was sleeping in the guest room. Over the years, I've watched you pretend to be happy even when I could see you were miserable—and lonely."

Unshed tears burned my eyes and my throat, and I fought them. My mother's addiction pushed her into despair, and I had a front row seat to her downward spiral. Bouts of depression. New baby. More liquor. Another kid. The cycle repeated. In between that, she cried. Every day. All day. And I never wanted my daughter to see me in that state. "Des, we don't have to talk about this now."

"I could hear you crying," Des confessed, tears streaming down her cheeks. "When you thought I was sleep."

My own tears burst free. Bliss was there with a box of Kleenex for both of us. "Thanks," I mumbled.

"Mom, you matter to me, too. I don't want you to fake happiness anymore." She grinned, even as her tears continued to fall. "It's time for you to have some fun."

I caressed her face. "I'm so proud of you, baby girl. Every day, you amaze me. I wouldn't be me if I wasn't your mother."

She blew out a breath. "And I wouldn't be so amazing if you weren't my mom. And if you want to make out with Mr. Spencer, then—"

"Wait," Blake sat up straight, tossing a balled-up piece of tissue into the small wastebin, "who the hell is Mr. Spencer?"

She glanced at Des. "And why the hell did you not lead with that? All this damn crying."

Bliss gaped, dabbing her wet eyes with Kleenex. "Right? 'Cause you've been holding out, Alaiya."

"Hell yeah," Dallas agreed, not even bothering to wipe off the evidence that she'd been crying, too. "Now, I have to fix my makeup."

"Y'all are wimps," Demi teased, her own voice shaky. "Get it together."

"For real," Blake said. "Duke is right. I'm soft."

"*You* definitely are," Dallas told Blake, ducking when a pillow whizzed past her head. Unfazed, she looked at me. "Okay, spill."

Closing my eyes, I tried to think of a way to cut this conversation short. But they were all staring at me, and they wouldn't let this go. "Making out implies that we were doing more than we were."

Dallas smirked. "What the hell were you doing?"

"It was a kiss," I admitted. "*One* kiss."

"A long kiss," Des murmured. "Anyway, I'm totally fine if you want to date Mr. Spencer."

"I still don't know who the hell Mr. Spencer is," Blake yelled. "Somebody say something."

Des laughed. "Blake, you're trippin'. My boss. Mr. Spencer?"

Demi frowned. "Taylar's uncle?"

"Zaddy!" Bliss beamed. "You kissed Zaddy."

Four pairs of wide eyes stared at me, making me extremely uncomfortable. I shifted, fidgeting with my sleeve. "Stop looking at me."

The corners of Blake's mouth quirked up. "Damn. You kissed fine-ass Spencer Cross."

Dallas gave her sister a high-five. "So fine."

"With his smooth, brown skin and beard," Bliss added.

A sly smile spread across Demi's mouth. "All that swag."

"Oh. My. God! Y'all are doing the most. Can we please not talk about this?" Des asked. "I'm okay with Mom dating him, but I don't need to know that Mr. Spencer is fine."

Bliss scoffed. "You have eyes, sweetie. You know a hottie when you see one."

Des bit down on her bottom lip. "Okay, he's handsome. In a fatherly way. Mom, if you like him, go for it."

A smile tugged at my lips as a huge wave a relief washed over me. Because now I was free to pursue this. And I wanted it. "Thanks, babe. What do you think?" I asked, twirling so they could see the fit.

"You're a snack." Des grinned. "And that outfit is snatched, Mom."

I gave her a hug. "Thanks, babe."

"Definitely," Dallas agreed. "I'm glad you chose a non-work option."

"Or funeral," Blake joked.

"Ha. Ha." I grabbed my coat. "I'm glad you came home, Des. But aren't you supposed to be helping Duke with the catering?"

My daughter had always marched to her own tune. Her college degree was merely a stepping stool in the grand scheme of her life. According to her, she wanted to thrive in her career, not simply survive. I'd always encouraged her to follow her own path, and in some ways, admired her for her commitment to self-fulfillment over upward mobility.

"Change of plans. Sloane decided to hire caterers," she explained. "She wanted Duke to enjoy the event, not worry about the food."

Demi gathered the empty wine glasses. "Which is good for me because I get to dance with my man and not play sous chef today. Duke was mad when she told him, though, because he doesn't trust other people's food."

I put my earrings in. "Makes sense. I don't either." Once I

was done with all the finishing touches, I turned to them again. "Okay, I'm ready."

"Do you have condoms?" Dallas asked.

"Really, Dallas?" Des screeched. "I don't need that visual."

"Better that than an oopsie baby," Bliss muttered.

I glared at my cousin. "Not a chance." I slipped on my boots, then my coat. Glancing at Dallas out of the corner of my eye, I said, "To answer your question, yes."

Des held her hands over her ears. "This is way more than I need to know."

"*But*," I checked my makeup in the mirror, "I won't need it tonight. We haven't even had a discussion yet. Besides, I just got divorced today."

"You haven't been fucked in at least a year, though," Blake interjected.

Des threw her hands up in frustration. "Why?"

I tossed a pillow at my cousin. "Shut. Up."

"I know you didn't just tell me to shut up," Blake tossed back.

"Sure did. I don't know why I tell you anything."

Blake shrugged. "Because you love me."

"You get on my damn nerves," I muttered. "I spoiled yo' little ass."

There was a ten-year age difference between us. When I first met Aunt Vicki, the twins were young. I wanted to get to know all of them, so I offered to babysit. Blake was attached to my hip, followed me everywhere. Watching my little cousins grow into adults, being such an important part of their lives, meant the world to me. I learned a lot from them. But damn … Blake never could keep her mouth shut.

"Yes, you did," Bliss chimed in. "You spoiled all of us. And we love you for it." She fixed the collar of my coat. "You smell good, you look good. Now you get to feel good."

Dallas snorted. "In a strictly dickly way."

We all laughed … even Des. While I knew it probably

wasn't a good time to get into something so serious, I was looking forward to the journey. Spence had checked off the first three items on my move-the-fuck-on list. Despite what I'd told the ladies, I couldn't deny the spark of hope in anticipation of number four—A LONG, HARD DICK.

As they filed out of the house ahead of me, I paused, hand on the door and an idea in my head. "Actually, why don't you all go ahead? I'll meet you there."

# CHAPTER 6

## *Can I Call You Rose?*

*Spencer*

"A re you in the hospital? 'Cause why the fuck are you FaceTiming me?"

My homeboy, Malcolm Jacobs, grinned widely. "I'm high as fuck right now, Ace Deuce."

He'd given me the nickname during a heated dice game after I won five racks rolling three on my first turn. And because my hometown, Ypsilanti, is close to Ann Arbor, which was affectionately referred to as Ace Deuce by people in the area.

Chuckling, I turned off my laptop. "And it's late, too," I added.

MJ took a hit from a joint. "Shit, I thought I was texting you."

Right after high school, I moved my Black ass down to Georgia with no plan. Learned a lot of hard lessons. I wasn't enrolled in school or anything, had no job, and didn't even care. My goal was to get the hell out of Michigan.

I met MJ when I dated his older sister, Monica. Got into some trouble because I didn't know when to stop talking shit. He had my back. Been fam ever since, even after I broke up with his sister.

MJ ran some of the biggest craps games in the country and owned a successful cannabis business. He was one of the main suppliers for the Leaf Lodge.

"What time is it there?" he asked.

I glanced at my watch. After spending most of my day putting out fires at work, I was running late for my nephew's engagement party. "Eight o'clock. What's good?"

"Shit," he grumbled, wiping his face. "This shit is weird as fuck. Video chatting." He barked out a laugh. "Looks like you're thinning up top, though."

"Shut the hell up, man."

"Might be time for you to go cut it all off." MJ's hairline had started receding early, and when he got tired of the jokes, he shaved his head bald. "Give it up."

*Time to steer this conversation to the matter at hand.* "I got shit to do. What's up, bruh?"

"Listen, a partner of mine got a lead on some property on the west side of your state, between Kalamazoo and Grand Rapids."

Curious, I asked, "Where at?"

"A town called Wellspring. Heard of it?"

"Yeah." When we were kids, my parents couldn't afford to take us on extravagant vacations, so we spent a lot of time on the road exploring Michigan. Wellspring was a small town, mostly Black population. Like Flint, their economy was tied to a major company, Wellspring Water Corporation. We'd driven through there several times but had never stayed longer than the few minutes it took to fill up the tank. I heard that they'd built the town up, but I still hadn't made a trip to visit. "What kind of property?"

"Used to be a retreat center. Several smaller cabins, a

common house, a few bungalows. Figured I'd toss the idea to you since you're diversifying your portfolio and delving more into hospitality."

My mind started turning with the possibilities. If the land was already zoned for a retreat with several different structures, it would be easier to develop it into what I needed. "How much land?"

"About a hundred and forty acres."

I didn't need to be convinced. I was already on it. "Send me the details, bruh."

My phone buzzed, and I glanced at the screen just in time to see an email notification. "Already done," he said. "Check your email."

"Good lookin'."

After opening the message, I scanned the attached document, made a few notes to myself while MJ informed me about the new product that he would be sending to me. Once I read everything, I forwarded a copy to Laiya. No time like the present to hop on a potential investment opportunity.

"You should receive your supply next week," MJ confirmed. "It's time to eat. Oh, Mo told me to tell you hi." He snickered. "She also told me she might leave her husband if you're interested."

Monica had kept in touch over the years, too. I'd managed to avoid her not-so-sly hints every time she messaged me on social media. She was nice, beautiful. But I learned fairly quickly we were not compatible. "Tell her to stay married."

MJ cracked up. "Bruh, don't do my sista like that."

A soft knock on my office door drew my attention away from the conversation. Everyone had gone home for the weekend, and I wasn't expecting anyone. Probably was the cleaning lady, but I never wanted to get caught slippin'. With my thumb, I flicked the safety off on the gun I kept on my hip. "Hold on, bruh. Yes," I called.

Alaiya peeked inside. "Hey. You busy?"

I motioned for her to come in. I peered at my phone. "Tell Mo I said what's up," I told MJ. "I'll keep you posted about that property."

Ending the call, I stood. "Aren't you supposed to be at the engagement party?"

She took her coat off and tossed it on an empty chair. But she didn't move. She simply stood at the door, her eyes locked on mine. "I wanted to talk to you."

Rounding my desk, I approached her. "Did something happen at court today?"

Alaiya flashed a grin. "That's why I'm here. To tell you I'm officially single."

I inched closer to her—until we were so close I could feel the rapid beat of her heart against my chest, smell the hint of mint on her breath. I didn't respond to her declaration. I just kissed her.

Her low groan as she wrapped her arms around my neck, leaning into me, giving herself and her mouth to me, nearly did me in. When she parted her lips, I dipped my tongue in her mouth. I reached behind her and turned the lock on the door.

*No interruptions.*

There was no space between us, but she still felt too far away from me. I pinned her against the door. I didn't give a damn about anything else in that moment but her. She'd offered me a slice of heaven that I never thought I'd reach, and I wanted to hold on to it. Forever.

*I can't let go.*

She moaned into my mouth, gripped my hair in her fist and tugged gently. "Spence," she breathed.

I trailed kisses down her chin, her neck, then back up to her earlobe. Nipping her tender skin, I murmured, "Yes."

"I thought we should talk."

I sunk my teeth into her shoulder, enjoying her sharp intake of breath. "What do you want to talk about?"

"I can't remember what I was going to say."

"You're divorced." I traced her bottom lip with my tongue, before placing a firm kiss to her mouth. "You're free to be mine."

"But ..." She whimpered when I sucked her lip into my mouth. "Oh God."

"Unless you're telling me no," I kissed the corners of her mouth, "I don't think there's anything left to say."

She cupped my jaw in her hand. "There are so many things that need to be said."

"Like?"

"First, I'm happy I'm not married to Rod anymore."

"Good."

She sucked in a deep breath. "But I'd be lying if I told you I wasn't scared of this thing between us. It's big. Hot and heavy. All-consuming. And I don't want to get hurt."

The vulnerability in her brown eyes made my heart clench in my chest. Because I would never intentionally hurt her. "I don't want you scared. I want you happy." I rested my forehead against hers. "Let *me* make you happy."

"I have walls. They're tall and wide. I'm good at keeping them up. I have so much baggage that I—"

I placed my forefinger against her mouth. "I don't need a history lesson on you. I've seen the parts of you that you think are ugly. Which is crazy to me because your past, your tenacity, your bravery in spite of everything stacked against you ... You see flaws, but I see beauty."

Her shoulders fell on a sigh. "You're good at this."

"I know what I want."

"Spence," she slowly unbuttoned my shirt, "I want you to take me out on a date."

I lifted a brow. "Is that all you want?"

Once she'd freed the last button, she slid my shirt off and smoothed her hand over my chest. "No. Before that, I want something else." She unbuckled my belt, unzipped my pants, and pushed them off. "Remember when you told me you'd give me anything I needed?"

I nodded. "I meant it."

Spinning around, she glanced back at me over her shoulder. "Help me out? Unzip me."

The sound of her zipper echoed in the office as my heart pounded loudly in my ears. Every inch of her brown skin was perfect. *She* was perfect. "So beautiful," I murmured against the nape of her neck.

When I finished, she turned to face me. "I need something, and only you can give it to me."

I snaked my arm around her waist, lifting her up. "Tell me what you need."

The corners of her mouth quirked up. "You read the list. I need a nigga," she slipped her hand into my boxers and squeezed my erection, "with a long, hard dick." She bit down on her lip. "Very impressive."

*Shit.* I carried her over to my desk and gently set her down. "I told you I got you."

Standing over her, I stared at her, letting my gaze roam over her bare skin. I feathered my fingers over her stomach, up to the front clasp of her bra. With my eyes on hers, I unhooked the latch. The black lace fell open, giving me my first glimpse of her breasts. *Perfect.* I bent to take one taut nipple in my mouth, sucking it while pinching the other with my fingers.

She purred. "Yes."

I tugged at the bottom of her jumpsuit, pulling it off and revealing her matching panties. I dragged my hands over her skin, down the waistband of her underwear. Her legs drifted apart, her unspoken request loud and clear. And I wanted to give her what she needed. Without warning, I ripped her panties off, smirking when her breath hitched.

"Spence," she groaned.

I held a finger up to my mouth, signaling for her to be

quiet just in case the cleaning crew was still in the building. "Are you sure you're ready for this?"

Another whimper escaped when I ran my finger over her pussy, massaging her clit with my finger. "Yes. Please."

Taking my finger, drenched with her arousal, I rubbed it over her lips before I sucked it into my mouth. Then, my mouth was on hers again, my tongue tangling with hers. I kissed my way down her body, closer to where I wanted to be. And just like I'd dreamed of doing for so long, I licked her from her clit to her entrance, dipping my tongue inside of her to sample more of her.

My desire to drive her crazy with need for me, to make her forget every disappointment, every ounce of pain she'd experienced, took over. My mission was to consume her, to conquer her, to make her dizzy in anticipation for the next time we could be like this with each other. Every time she took a breath, I wanted her to think about me. Every time she showered, I wanted her to imagine me behind her, washing her from head to toe.

I couldn't get enough of her, of her taste, of her low moans, of her whispered pleas. I was relentless, teasing her with my mouth, my tongue, enjoying the way she whispered my name over and over.

When I sucked her clit into my mouth, Laiya shattered as an orgasm ripped through her, and I swallowed up her cries with a kiss. But I wasn't done with her. I wanted more. I slid one finger—then two—inside of her heat and started the dance again, winding her up until she came again on my tongue.

At this point, my dick was begging for mercy. I was so hard, so ready to take her, to make her mine. *Damn*. I paused at her entrance, waited a heartbeat before inching inside.

"*Shit*," I hissed, clenching my jaw.

She was warm, so tight. And I was done—all hers. No

question. Because I would be no good for anyone else after this.

"Oh God," she breathed. "So good."

I rested my body on hers, brushed my lips over her mouth. I traced the curve of her nose. "You're so beautiful."

Her eyes popped open. "You make me feel this beautiful."

"I don't want to stop."

"Then don't," she said.

I started moving, slow and easy. The rhythm was innate, natural. Pushing and pulling. Taking and giving. Like we were meant for this moment, meant to be this way. Feeling her around me felt right. We clung to each other, taking our time to explore, to touch, to taste. Laiya had seized control over every inch of my body as pleasure threatened to choke me with its intensity.

Soon, the need to complete eclipsed my desire to prolong this and I picked up the pace. Harder. Faster. Then slower, softer. Alaiya met me with each thrust. Tingling in my thighs signaled it wouldn't be long before my legs gave out, but she was close. I was, too.

When she came, with my name on her lips, it was glorious —the most beautiful sight I'd ever seen. A sensation I'd never felt before coated my stomach, crept down my spine, seeped into my bones, and settled in my heart. *Love.* That realization was enough to send me over the edge as my own orgasm ripped through me, wringing me dry and cementing that this was the only way I wanted to spend the rest of my life. *In her arms.*

WHEN WE FINALLY ARRIVED AT the Smoke and Burn Lounge for the engagement party, I could hear the music, the laughter, and the conversation from outside. I reached out to open the door, but Alaiya's hand on mine stopped me.

Turning to her, I asked, "What's wrong?"

She shook her head. "We can't go in there."

I brushed a strand of hair out of her face. "Why?"

"Because we're three hours late," she whispered.

After we left my office, I followed her home, jumped in the shower with her, helped her get dressed—then *un*dressed again. I was perfectly fine with skipping the party, but Laiya insisted we show our faces. Mostly because we both had received several calls from various family members wondering where the hell we were.

"What's your hesitation?" I brushed my lips over her brow. "Because we were on the same page a few minutes ago."

"I don't know." She nibbled on her thumbnail. "The way my hair looks like I been getting dicked down ..." She flattened a hand over her stomach. "It's obvious we've been together."

Amused, I asked, "You think so?"

She smirked. "Well, you can't seem to stop touching me."

Holding her face in my hands, I kissed her eyes, both of her cheeks, her chin, and finally her mouth. "Guilty."

"And I just got divorced this afternoon," she pointed out.

"Isn't that good news?"

"Of course. But you know how people talk. Tomorrow, the whole city will think we've been fucking around for years."

"Anyone who knows us, will know that's not true."

She wrapped her arms around my waist. "I know I shouldn't care what people think, but I do."

"I get it. So how about this? You walk in the front door, and I'll go through the back."

"You would do that for me?"

I lifted her chin with my forefinger. "Do you even have to ask?"

Grinning, she pressed her mouth to mine. "I—"

"Ooo!"

Our gazes snap toward the door where the bride- and groom-to-be stood.

"I'm telling," Sloane teased, a mischievous smirk on her face. "Wait 'til Courtney hears about this." She waved at me. "Hi, Uncle Spence." Then, she bolted inside.

Laiya cursed. "Sloane, wait. Shit." She rushed into the building after her cousin.

Inside the lounge, I peeped Alaiya dragging Sloane toward the back of the bar. Chuckling to myself, I said, "Never a dull moment."

"What's up?" Maddox approached me and gave me a dap. "You made it."

"Wouldn't miss it," I told him.

He raised a questioning brow. "Really?"

Ignoring him, I clasped his shoulder and squeezed. "Congrats, nephew. I'm happy for you. I know it's been tough the last few years."

He smiled. "Yeah, but Sloane makes everything better. Listen, Unc, I was going to ask you … I would love it if you were my best man."

Maddox was conceived when my brother, Ryan, and his wife were separated. Growing up, he'd struggled to find his place in the family. I'd experienced the same feelings because of the age gap between me and my siblings and made it a point to reach out to him, to make myself available if he needed me. Even though he grew up on the East Coast with his mother, we'd maintained a close bond. I was extremely happy that he'd finally found someone. To hear that he wanted me to stand up with him was an honor.

"What about Ryker?" I asked.

"According to Sloane, Keon bought Taylar a ring. I figured I'd let him off the hook for this wedding. He'll still be a groomsman, though."

I nodded. "Ah, gotcha." I couldn't help but be proud that I got to watch my nieces and nephews come into their own, that I was able to witness them realize their dreams. "Whatever you need, nephew. I'm there."

Maddox smiled, giving me a quick hug. "Thanks, Unc. Appreciate it."

Several minutes later, we stepped into the building. The place was jam packed with people. Which wasn't surprising since Sloane and Maddox came from pretty big extended families. There were Youngs and Crosses everywhere. But my eyes were fixated on one person.

Alaiya was seated near the bar. She was talking to her aunt and uncle, Vicki and Stew Young. The smile on her face told me she was more at ease than she was outside, so I stopped to talk to my siblings. Life was busy for all of us, and it was rare that we were in the same place at the same time. But when we saw each other, it was all love. I would've sat with them a while longer if Sabrina hadn't attempted to introduce me to her single friend.

Excusing myself, I made a beeline toward Laiya. On my way to her, I chopped it up with several people who I hadn't seen in years, dodged a distant cousin who'd sent me a business proposal the other day, and another woman who'd requested a meeting to discuss one of the properties that I'd already told her I wasn't willing to sell. Near the buffet, I noticed Sloan, Courtney, and Vicki's daughters exchanging knowing glances at each other.

*I guess Sloane made good on her threat.*

Someone tapped my shoulder, and I turned to find Des standing behind me, a tentative smile on her face. "What's up, Des?"

She shrugged. "Hey, Mr. Spence. Got a minute?"

"Sure." After Des walked in on me kissing Laiya, she'd pretty much avoided me at work. And I didn't push. "You okay?"

"I will be. I just wanted to say … I'm my mom's person. And she's mine. She is very important to me."

"I understand. We have that in common."

Her shoulders fell. "She deserves nothing more than all the happiness she can stand. I hope you can give that to her."

I smiled. "Does this mean you're okay with me dating your mother?"

Sighing, she said, "If I said no, would you back off?"

"Is that what you're saying?"

"No, I'm not. And I'm okay with it—*only* if you promise to treat her well." She jabbed a finger into my chest. "Don't make me fight you," she warned, a gleam in her eyes. "'Cause I will."

I laughed. "You won't have to. Des, I hope you know that I want the same things for her that you do."

Surprising me, she gave me a hug. "I believe you," she whispered. "Alright, you can go to her. Sloane already told all your business. Mom might look like she's smiling, but deep inside, she's flipping out."

"Thanks for letting me know."

Before I walked away, Des shared an idea she had for National Weed Day, April 20th. I told her to put a meeting on my calendar so we could discuss the details, then joined Alaiya at the bar.

Her eyes lit up. "Spence. You finally made it over here."

Leaning closer, I whispered, "Sloane busted us, didn't she?"

"Like only she could," she mumbled.

I eyed the empty shot glass on the bar top. "What are you drinking?"

"Shot of tequila. My nerves are bad …"

After waving the bartender over, I placed an order. When he returned with two full shot glasses, I handed her one. We toasted to minding our business and took our shots.

Scowling, she set her glass down. "Yuck. Still nasty."

I scanned the room. "Nice party."

She nodded. "Yeah."

While the music was hype and the crowd was lively, I was more interested in peeling Laiya's clothes off and burying myself inside of her again. "You ready to go?"

Grinning, she hopped off the barstool. "I been ready. Your place or mine?"

"Mine." Unfazed by the curious glances and the not-so-quiet whispers, I entwined my fingers with hers, kissed the inside of her wrist, and led her out of the bar.

# CHAPTER 7
## You're Making Me High

*Alaiya*

My relationship with sex was complicated. I lost my virginity at sixteen to one of my brother's friends. Gerald Lewis. As with most of my childhood, my mother was nowhere around, and we were left to our own devices. This particular night, my older siblings had thrown a house party, complete with liquor, weed, and debauchery.

In hindsight, it was one of those times I wished I could take back. Not for the reasons most would think, though. He sucked, but I did, too. I was completely out of my depth in the ways a person can give and receive pleasure. It was almost mechanical—insert dick here, make obnoxious grunting sounds, two pumps, then it was over. Less than a minute of absolute hell.

All I could remember thinking was, *Is this it*?

Unfortunately, it was. Gerald had rolled off the bed, removed his condom, tucked his little thing in his pants, and strolled out to rejoin the party. And I was lying on top of an unmade bed, staring at the ceiling and questioning my life choices.

After that experience, I vowed to never waste my time again. Until I met Rod. Our lovemaking was soft and sweet, not rushed. He was romantic and he tried his best in the beginning. I enjoyed it, but there always seemed to be something missing. Passion? Abandon? As the years passed, our sex life morphed from a loving moment between us to a consistent routine. Almost like a task, something to check off every week. I could count on one hand the number of times I'd been so spent that I collapsed on the bed, struggling to catch my breath. Because that didn't happen. Instead of going back for seconds, we each disappeared into our own bubble of responsibilities. Work. Parenting. Bills. Appearances.

Now I found myself in a different, yet welcome predicament. I'd never had so much sex in a thirty-day period as I'd had with Spence the past month.

Any time of the day.

Every surface we could find.

All the positions.

So many orgasms.

*And I want more.*

I wanted everything. All of him. All day. Every day. He'd taken a pickaxe to my brick walls, and they were crumbling at a rapid pace. He'd opened Pandora's box, and I couldn't go back to life without *this*, without his arms around me, without his lips on me, without his body against mine.

The scariest part of this whole thing? That he'd leave me a fiend, unable to escape my need for him. *I might be addicted to the long, hard dick.* Even now, after three orgasms, I found myself burrowing into him, silently begging him to make me come. Again.

His fingers gripped my hips, his nose brushed the back of my neck, his teeth sunk into my skin, and his low voice filtered to my ears. "I can't get enough of you."

"Same," was my one-word reply as he pressed his erection against my pussy. In one fluid movement, he inched inside of me, filling me so completely it took my breath away.

He didn't move for what felt like an eternity, and I was good with it for now. I just wanted him close to me, inside of me. Being together like this was the icing on a moist, delicious cake. Almost forty years of friendship—acceptance, understanding, stimulating conversations, shared goals. The things that were already there between us were coupled with a soul searing, uncontrollable passion.

The moment I'd cracked the door open, he'd stepped in like he always belonged there. *In some ways, he did.*

Spence muttered filthy, dirty words as he pulled out slowly, then hammered into me.

*I love it.*

Cursing, he gripped my chin, craned my head to the side, and kissed me.

*Oh God, I love this, too.* The sex was amazing, but he knew how to command my mouth, too—with the right amount of tongue and teeth.

So hot.

Masterful.

*I'm here for it.*

We made love as the world around us faded away. The countless meetings scheduled, house showings on the calendar, and the obligations that needed to be met were a distant second to this. My senses were reserved for him. I could see, hear, feel, smell, and taste nothing but him. Our reflection in the long mirror on the wall, the way he whispered my name as if I was the answer to his prayers, his hard chest against my back, the scent of his soap, the hint of cool mint mixed with coffee on his breath.

The pace quickened as I continued to surrender myself to him—longer, faster, harder. I was close. So close. "Spence," I pleaded. "Please."

"It's okay, baby. Come for me."

Three words. Desired effect. My orgasm took over, pulsing through me, spreading from my core through every part of my body. Then, he followed me over, pressing his mouth to mine as he succumbed to his own climax.

Moments later, when my heart was no longer beating out of my chest and I could breathe normally again, I shifted to face him. I closed my eyes as he traced my nose, my lips, the line of my jaw with his finger. "I'm probably never going to stop wanting this," I admitted, searching his eyes.

He smirked. "That's the plan."

"You had a plan?"

"You're not the only one with a list."

One of the things I loved about Spencer was that he was old school. Although he used technology at work, he valued paper and pen. "Tell me more."

Bending down, he licked my nipple, circling it with his tongue before sucking it into his mouth. When he let it go with a pop, he said, "Spencer's Help-Alaiya-Move-The-Fuck-On List."

I giggled. "Are you serious?"

*I love this.* For the first time in my life, I felt cherished. The last several weeks had been a whirlwind of activity. Work had picked up for both of us, so we took advantage of every free moment. Spencer had spoiled me with dates and weekend getaways. But my favorite times with him were the quiet nights we spent at his place, wrapped up in each other, reminiscing about the good times and sharing our hopes for the future.

He tucked a piece of hair behind my ear. "Mostly."

Perching myself up on my elbow, I asked, "What's number one?"

"That's easy. I put you to work so you could get that money."

I couldn't help the smile that spread across my face. "You definitely did that."

Even before the New Year, he'd lined up several projects, and he hadn't stopped sending them. In fact, we were currently in Wellspring, Michigan, trying to close a deal on a new property. And I would continue working my ass off to ensure we both increased our bottom line. Not just because of the money, but because I believed in his mission.

"My list is basically a response to yours," he explained. "Help with the purge, provide the drink and the edible. Which you fucked up."

My head fell against his chest as my cheeks burned with embarrassment. I hadn't been able to live that down. Des brought it up often. "Can we please forget that happened? My nose is back on my face, and everything is its regular size. It's behind me. Finally." I cuddled into him, humming when he wrapped his arms around me. "Next."

"I'm your nigga."

I snorted, bursting out in an uncontrollable fit of laughter, until tears of mirth spilled down my cheeks. "I still can't believe it wrote that down."

He cracked up, rubbing my face. "Honestly, I can't believe it either."

"I wish I could've saw your face when you read it."

The rumble of his laughter made me feel centered, content. I loved to hear him laugh. He had a good one. "The best thing about that list was that it shifted my perspective."

"About me?"

Spence smoothed his hand down my back, cupping my ass with his palm and pulling me closer. "About *us*. Possibilities."

I sighed, hooking my leg over his hip. "I like that. Must've been destiny."

"And vibes. Because we always had the vibes."

A smile tugged at my lips. "That's facts. Is that it?"

"There was one additional item."

"Tell me."

"Not now."

I peered up at him. "Is it bad?"

"Nah, but it's not the right time."

"Uh oh," I grumbled. "That sounds scary."

"Don't be scared, Laiya," he assured. "You'll know soon enough."

We lay there in silence for a few moments as the haze of desire, the ease of our conversation morphed into something else. Fear. It wasn't a new emotion. It had crept in often, usually when I felt happy, safe. Like the bottom would fall out and I would be left careening into a dark abyss. Yes, my imagination has always been a little dark.

"Spencer?" I called.

He kissed the top of my head. "Yes."

"Do you think this is too fast?"

Pulling back, he searched my eyes. "Why? Do you have any regrets?"

I hunched a shoulder. "Not so much regret, but concerns. Mostly, I've tried to be careful. Except when I was being reckless. But those times were few and far between. When I'm with you, though, I feel like I'm losing control."

"And *that* scares you."

"Kind of," I confessed. "We're not that young."

"Speak for yourself," he joked. "I'm just getting started."

I shoved him playfully. "I'm serious. I'm in the latter half of my forties. And you're …"

He narrowed his eyes on me. "Watch it," he warned.

I grinned. "You're Zaddy."

"That's right." He pulled me back to him. "I'm *your* Zaddy."

"True." I gave him a quick kiss. "Anyway, we've both lived separate lives. I'm just saying … it might not be as easy as it feels right now to be together long term. You know as

well as I do that the honeymoon phase ends quickly sometimes. Then you're left with a reality you might not have
chosen for yourself if you could see into the future."

He sat up, leaning back against the headboard. My
stomach fell as dread welled up inside. He entwined his
fingers with mine and stared at our joined hands. "Laiya, I'm
not confused about how I feel about you. I'm just waiting on
you to catch up."

I blinked. "What?"

Spence chuckled. "This is not a bad thing, baby."

"It doesn't sound good," I tossed back.

"It's all about perspective. I've been through a lot, done a
lot of shit I'm not proud of, and lost people that I thought
would be around."

My shoulders fell. Spencer was close to his parents, and
he'd lost both within a few years of each other. That had to be
hard on him.

"I learned from mistakes and used my experiences to be
better. We've already established that, if we could go back, we
might make different choices. Nothing has changed and I'm
not going back on my word."

I brought his palm up to my lips and kissed it softly.
"You're one of the best people I know, Spence. I married Rod
because he was my best friend and look where we are. If
something happens, if this doesn't work, I don't want to lose
you."

"Do you trust me?"

Without hesitation, I nodded my head. "Yes."

"Why?"

My brows drew down in confusion. "What do you
mean?"

"Why do you trust me?" he pressed. "Is it because I've
been there for you?"

"That's part of it, but … I trust you because you're you."

"Exactly. And I trust you to be who you are."

"Is that enough, though?" I tossed back. "Is our past enough to build a future?"

"That's part of the journey. As long as we understand each other, remain open with each other, and take it one day at time, we'll be fine."

"You really believe that?"

He bumped his shoulder with mine. For some reason, that simple gesture settled the doubt threatening to burst our perfect bubble. It was a signal, one that meant he was there for me, that he had my back, and that I didn't have to worry. He'd done it on the playground after he gave me his lunch, and he'd done it so many times since. Before, I took it as a confirmation of our friendship, but now it felt like a promise. His commitment to remain the person I've always known him to be.

"You know I do," he whispered.

I swallowed through a wave of dueling emotions. When we were together, when he was making love to me, I could forget my doubts, lose myself in him. Yet, as much as I wanted this, I couldn't turn off the part of me that was terrified it would destroy us.

Spence tipped my chin up, touching his mouth to mine in a chaste kiss. "Baby, I do know you, and I understand that you need to be sure about us. We can go as slow as you need. Because I'm here, and I'm not going anywhere. Never doubt that."

Allowing myself to give in to my feelings was a huge risk. The pieces of my life had been held together by shreds of tape and thin threads of fabric for so long. Yet, with every passing day, a small part of me healed. A lot of that had to do with Spence. And even though the fear was there, I knew one thing for sure …

*I don't want to let this go.*

———

*A couple weeks later*

"HEY, BABE."

There was something about Aunt Vicki's voice that always calmed my nerves. I couldn't help but smile as I bent to hug her before taking my seat across from her. "Hi. Sorry I'm late."

My last meeting had lasted longer than expected. Mostly because the seller wanted to review every line item on the purchase agreement. And because he commanded me to hop on his dick. Which was why Spence was my favorite client.

"You're fine," she assured.

Glancing around the restaurant, I asked, "Is Uncle Linc coming?"

She tipped her head toward the back of the place. "He'll be right back. Went to the restroom." She leaned forward, resting her elbows on the table. "I'm a little surprised you wanted him to join us today."

Honestly, I was, too. Typically, our lunch dates were reserved for me and her. But things had changed so drastically in a matter of months, I felt the need to touch base with two of the most important people in my life. "I just wanted to spend some time with both of you."

She seemed to accept that answer because she smiled. "That's nice."

Uncle Linc joined us. "Hey, niece." He kissed my brow and slid into the booth next to me.

We spent a few minutes catching up, mostly talking about the upcoming wedding. It was good to see Uncle Linc excited about something. He'd always been pretty stoic, and I knew it was because he'd been through so much. My uncle had the distinction of being the only member of my family that survived his battle against addiction. It took him losing his wife and kids for a time, but he'd fought for the life he wanted and won. I admired him so much.

I sighed wistfully. "I'm happy for Sloane and Maddox. And you, Uncle Linc."

He wrapped his arm around my shoulder and squeezed tightly. "Thanks, Laiya. I told Sloane she might have to hold me up while we're walking down the aisle."

Aunt Vicki patted his hand. "You'll be fine, Linc. Just remember … married or not, she'll still need you. And she'll steal your food when she visits, call at all times of the night to ask questions about random stuff, and drop her babies off and run out before you can catch her."

Uncle Linc raised a brow. "Babies?"

Laughing, I asked, "Let me guess … Dallas?"

"Chile, yes," Aunt Vicki confirmed.

"I thought you knew something I didn't." Uncle Linc chuckled, sipping his coffee.

My aunt shook her head. "As far as I know, Sloane isn't pregnant. But Blake? She might be."

I slapped my hand on the table. "I knew it."

"She still hasn't said anything yet," she said. "But I have a feeling somebody is pregnant."

The waitress returned with our food. After a few minutes, I announced, "I'm seeing someone." My aunt and uncle paused, forks midair. "I know it's soon after the divorce, but I just wanted you to know."

"Babe, we already know about you and Spencer."

I gaped. *I'ma slap Sloane.* "Who told you?"

My uncle snickered. "You and Spencer. When y'all walked out of the engagement party forty minutes after you arrived … three hours late."

A blush worked its way up my neck, and I ducked my head, pushing my salad around my plate. "Point taken."

"You know I'm not surprised," Aunt Vicki said. "But I'm glad you're finally letting yourself explore it."

"I like him a lot."

Aunt Vicki pinned me with her gaze. "You *like* him?"

Shifting in my seat, I scratched the back of my neck. "I might feel more for him than like."

"Might?" Uncle Linc tag teamed.

"No, I do," I admitted.

He set his fork down. "What's the problem?"

"Is it too soon? After the divorce." It had been a few weeks since we'd had the discussion. Spence had assured me we could go slow, but everything between us happened super fast. Married to Rod one day, dicked down by Spence the next.

"Laiya, I get it." Aunt Vicki set her glass of water down. "You spent decades in a marriage that didn't fulfill you. It's natural for you to feel hesitant about starting something new. But let the record show … what's happening between you and Spencer is *not* new. I'm a witness."

Uncle Linc nodded. "Exactly."

Frowning, I glanced at him. "You weren't there, Uncle."

"*That* day," he said. "I've seen you with him."

My mind drifted back to the only time I'd run into my uncle when I was with Spence before the divorce. We'd met for lunch at Coney Island to discuss real estate. Ran into Uncle Linc and Aunt Layla. "We were talking business."

"But there was a comfort between you that I've never seen with you and Rod."

*Wow.* "That's deep."

Aunt Vicki squeezed my hand. "Babe, when you think of your life at fifty—"

I jerked back in surprise. "That's a few years away," I pointed out.

"I know, Alaiya. You don't have to remind me. Just go with it."

"Okay."

"Visualize who's sitting next to you," she continued.

"You're having fun, laughing, talking, just enjoying your time. Who's with you?"

It didn't take much to imagine the scene. A beach or a porch. A gentle breeze. Stillness. His smile … "Spence," I whispered.

Aunt Vicki passed a knowing glance to Uncle Linc before her eyes connected with mine. "That's what I thought. Stop thinking about the timing. The important thing to remember is that you're single. He's single. You're free to be with each other."

"Spence said the same thing."

"He's smart," Uncle Linc said. "When I fell in love with Layla, I knew within minutes I wanted to spend the rest of my life with her."

"You two have had decades to figure it out," Aunt Vicki added.

"You're right," I conceded.

"Good," she chirped. "Our work here is done. Just don't elope this time."

I giggled, shaking my head. "I don't think you have to worry about that any time soon."

While I hadn't considered marrying again, I couldn't help but feel excited about the vision of the future I'd conjured up. Living carefree with Spencer. For the rest of our lives.

# CHAPTER 8

*Vibe for Me*

*Spencer*

The Annual Ann Arbor Hash Bash took place on the first Saturday in April. Vendors from all over descended on University of Michigan's campus for the free festival. Throughout the day, attendees listened to speeches from cannabis activists, local politicians, and special-interest groups. My brother, Ryan, in his role as a U.S. Rep, was on the program as well.

This year, Des had convinced me to sign on as a vendor at a related event known as the Monroe Street Fair. I'd been on site since noon, passing out flyers and telling people about The Leaf Lodge. Des had joined me, taking reservations for weekend stays and selling tickets to our first 420 Puff-n-Paint event.

"This is amazing," she said, waving at a few passersby as they browsed the various tables. "So many people."

The smell of bud and food permeated the air, while live music filtered to our ears from the sound stage. It was a festive occasion, one that I had attended several times since I was a teenager. "It's definitely an experience."

"Maybe one day soon I can have a food truck out here," she mused. "That would be a dream come true."

I glanced at her. "You already have your business plan. You can make it work."

"There's so much I want to do. I want to go out on my own, but I also love the work I'm doing for you."

"You have choices. Even if you decide to do your own thing, you can always come back and do events for me. Or whatever you want to do."

She smiled sweetly at me. "You've been good to me, Spence."

Since I'd started seeing Alaiya, Des had finally stopped calling me Mr. Spence. While I appreciated that she'd always considered it a show of respect, it made me feel like her grandfather. I was glad when the change happened. "The feeling is mutual. I would hate to lose you."

She smiled. "You won't. Especially since you're dating my mom." She chewed on her thumbnail. It was a quirk she got from her mother. "I love that you make her so happy. I've never seen her smile this much. When she wasn't with me," she added.

I barked out a laugh. "Good to know."

"If you want to move in, I'm perfectly willing to rent one of your houses so that you two can be alone."

Smiling, I asked, "Is that a hint?"

"Maybe. I overheard you and Mom talking about one of your tenants moving out."

Construction on the homes I'd purchased in December would be complete by June. Last week, the purchase agreement was signed, and one of my long-term tenants would soon become a homeowner. "And you're ready to move out?"

"I'm not gonna lie … I'm nervous. But my best friend is looking for a place, too. I figured we could share the expenses." She ticked off the things she'd done to prepare for a move —six months of rent saved, credit cards paid off, an additional savings account for furniture and other things she would need when she got her own place. "And I have a working budget."

The more she talked, the more she sounded like Alaiya. And me. *She should've been my daughter*. It wasn't the first time I'd thought that, and probably wouldn't be the last.

"I searched up the house," she continued. "It's close to Mom, which is ideal because I'll still need her. *And* … I think I would be the perfect tenant. You know me, you trust me."

I pretended to mull it over for a moment. Then I said, "Call my office on Monday. We can talk about it."

Des jumped up and gave me a hug. "Thanks, Spence." She whipped out her phone, typing furiously on the screen. "I have to tell Cee."

When she walked away, I started organizing the table and replenishing the flyers and information sheets before the second shift got here. My phone buzzed.

LAIYA

How long are you going to be there?

Half an hour. You miss me?

LAIYA

I need your assistance with something.

What's up? You good?

LAIYA

I'm perfect. Come to my place when you're done?

I sent a message to the manager coming to relieve us, asking for an estimated ETA. When he responded and said he was parking his car, I told Laiya:

Be there in a little bit.

———

"Happy Birthday, baby!"

Alaiya stood in the middle of the room, holding a small cake and wearing nothing but a paper hat.

Smiling, I approached her. "You didn't have to do this, Laiya." I dipped my finger into the icing and tasted it. Then, I repeated the motion, this time spreading a thin layer of frosting across her lips and kissing her, long and hard. "That's good."

She set the cake down and stepped closer, standing on her toes and pressing her mouth on mine. "Should we cut a piece?" She yelped when I lifted her in a fireman's carry. "Spence!"

I smacked her ass lightly. "I'd rather you let me fuck you."

She screamed with delight when I dropped her on the mattress. "I'm good with that," she said, tugging me on top of her.

I pulled my shirt off while she unbuttoned my pants, pushing them off with her feet. Then, my mouth was on her pussy, sucking on her clit, bringing her to the brink of an orgasm before I flipped her over and entered her from behind.

*Damn.* She always felt good. And she was so wet for me, so ready to get fucked. And I was ready to give her what she needed. We didn't waste time as we raced to bliss. It didn't take long either, because she growled out her release mere seconds before my own orgasm nearly split me in half with its intensity. When my breathing slowed down, I rolled onto my back, pulling her on top of me.

She glanced up at me, nipped my chin, then sucked my bottom lip into her mouth. "Now when you think of your birthday, you can think of me."

I kissed her. "Thanks for this."

"I know it's a hard day for you."

My father and I shared the same birthday. Every year, we would spend the day together. Pop worked as a mechanic until he retired, so his idea of fun was tinkering in the garage. And he was proud of his skill, often drawing diagrams to demonstrate how the various parts worked. He'd taught me the difference between a spark plug and a serpentine belt, how to change tires and check the oil, and when to replace worn-out brake pads. Dad was practical. He'd only bought me three gifts in my life—a small tool kit to keep in my car, a set of jumper cables, and a can of WD-40 lubricant in case I had trouble loosening a lug nut. And, yes, he put that gift in a box and set it under the tree at Christmas. I never cared, though. I just soaked it all up.

After he died, my birthdays weren't the same. April 6th became just another day. Today was no different. I woke up, pried myself out of Alaiya's bed, and went to work. I forgot it was my birthday … until she called and sang the birthday song in the silliest, but cutest rendition I'd ever heard. And when she asked me to stop for lunch I hadn't hesitated.

"Dad would've loved you," I told her.

"I remember your dad. He gave me a snow shovel one day."

I chuckled. "He did?"

"It was right when I started driving. I had that old hooptie."

"And the door wouldn't stay closed."

"Exactly," she said. "Anyway, I got stuck at the corner by your parents' house. He must've seen me from the window because he came out and helped me clean off my car. Then, he gave me the shovel."

"Sounds like something he would do."

"Spence, I didn't have good parents. Didn't know my father. Couldn't stand my mother. They never gave me anything but heartbreak. Your father's kind gesture meant the world to me. So much that I kept that snow shovel for years."

"I'm glad he helped you."

"Just like his son did."

"I miss him," I admitted as tears burned the back of my throat. "That's why I don't make a big deal about my birthday."

"Well, from now on, you should. You deserve to be celebrated. Your parents are gone, but you were a good son to them. You're an amazing, present uncle. And you support your siblings. Sabrina told me about your donation to her event."

I groaned. "She can't hold water."

"She's proud of you. I am, too. You are blessed, Spence. And you're a *blessing* to everyone you care about. So I don't give a damn what you say. It's all about you today, baby."

Wrapping my arms around her, I hugged her, taking the comfort she provided. It hadn't been two months, but she'd given me more during this short time than I'd received in five years of marriage.

We stayed in the rest of the day. Alaiya stayed true to her word, making the entire day about me. She'd cooked my favorite dinner and two pans of cornbread. Then, we ate together while we binged the entire *John Wick* series. After the first movie, she took my dick in her mouth. When the second movie ended, I fucked her against the cool tile while we showered. During part three, we made love while John killed off the High Table enforcers. Finally, once the final duel ended in the last movie, Alaiya climbed on my dick and rode me until we fell over together.

I nuzzled her hair. "Baby?"

"Hm?"

"Thanks for making this the best birthday I've ever had."

"You're welcome, baby." She kissed my chest. "Wait 'til next year. I already have plans."

The room descended into silence for a moment. Her breathing slowed down, and I knew she would soon drift off to sleep. "Remember when I told you I had another item on my list?"

She glanced at me with hooded eyes. "Yes."

Reaching over to the nightstand, I grabbed my wallet and pulled out a Post-it note. I handed it to her. "This is my list."

Laiya sat up, not bothering to cover her naked skin. She pushed her hair back from in front of her eyes and read it aloud. "Number six. Tell Alaiya I …" Gasping, she turned to me. "When did you write this?"

"I added it on the day you took that edible. And I knew for sure after the first time we made love."

She bit down on her bottom lip. "But, how?"

I dragged a finger down her cheek, then tugged her to me. "It is what it is," I murmured against her mouth. "What it probably has always been."

Tears filled her eyes. "Then say it."

While she was sleeping off her high, I realized that my desire for her was more than simple attraction. It was more than sex. It had everything to do with the connection we'd always shared. That was the day I knew that I loved her.

"I love you, Laiya," I whispered.

A slow smile spread over her lips. "Uncle Linc told me he fell in love with Aunt Layla the first day he met her. To some it might seem preposterous. But to me … it felt like a confirmation. You told me we could go slow, but I think it was already too late. Because I was enamored with you from the moment you ignored the fact that I had on a hot-ass Wonder Woman costume in the middle of the summer."

I laughed, even as my heart pounded in my ears.

"And that feeling never really went away. No matter how much I ran from it. Even when both of us tried to ignore it." The tips of her fingers drifted across my cheek, and she kissed me. "Spencer, I love you, too."

Those three words, coupled with the emotion in her eyes, nearly wrecked me. In the best way. Nothing had ever felt like this. I wasn't sure what I did to deserve her, but I would make sure I spent the rest of my life showing her how much she meant to me.

I turned us over, resting my body on top of hers. "I want to always be like this with you."

She wrapped her legs around my waist. "I'm good with that."

Later, as we laid in each other's arms, after I made her come on my tongue, I thought back to the end of last year. If I hadn't been sitting with Yolanda at that speed dating event, Laiya wouldn't have felt the need to intervene with Taylar. If she hadn't intervened, I probably wouldn't have seen her move-on plan. Circumstances brought us together, but that list changed everything. Now, I was here with her, looking forward to building a life together. The way it was always meant to be.

*Epilogue*

4EVERMORE

*Spencer*

*Four20, One Year Later*

The intoxicating scent of roses and weed surrounded us as we stared up at the stars. The Leaf Lodge had officially expanded to Wellspring, Michigan. Hosting the opening on National Weed Day was a no brainer and we decided to make it a weekend event. Currently, our family and friends were enjoying the inaugural *Hiy*Vibe Event.

The best part? I didn't have to do anything. Des and Taylar handled the planning, the décor, the food, and the itinerary for the weekend. Tonight, guests dressed to impress in all black while they sampled cannabis-infused dishes, danced to old school R&B and hip hop, and enjoyed the grounds. Scattered around the room were DIY stations that offered everything from pre-rolls and joint rolling demonstrations to bong carts and CBD mocktails.

"Do you think they'll miss us?"

Turning my head to Laiya, I held the rose blunt to her mouth and smiled when she inhaled. We'd slipped out of the party before dessert. The moonlit walk was a welcome reprieve from all the activity. "Nah," I answered, taking a hit.

A slow smile spread across her lips. "Des would flip out if she knew I was smoking this blunt with you."

I brought her hand up to my mouth, placing a kiss to her soft skin. "It's our secret." In the past year, I'd come to enjoy the simple act of being quiet with my lady, spending time reading, playing cards, watching television, making love. If I could die in her arms, I would consider myself blessed beyond measure.

"We have a lot of those," she mused, sliding over to my lap and burrowing into my chest—right where I wanted her.

The stillness of the night, the soft breeze, and the bud lulled me into a relaxed state. Our bungalow was situated on the far end of the property, but I could hear the faint sounds of music. Laiya hummed along to the tune.

"I'm okay with not going back," she announced.

I chuckled. "It was a wrap the minute I walked out."

Giggling, she shifted in my arms, brushed her mouth over my jawline, then nipped my chin. "I love you for that."

"Is that all you love me for?" I kissed her, sucking her bottom lip into my mouth. "Because I know how to dip out of an event without goodbyes?"

"I still don't know how you can just walk away without closing the conversation." Alaiya had shed a lot of her old quirks when we decided to be together, but she'd always been way too polite. Every interaction needed a warm greeting or sincere farewell.

"You didn't grow up with Sabrina as your sister."

She cracked up. "Right? She's a trip. I'm surprised she came."

I snickered. "I'm not. She never turns down an edible."

"She's better than me," she grumbled. "Never again."

"You said the same thing about smoking," I reminded.

"It's different with you, though." She circled my nose with hers. "Everything is different with you." She linked her fingers with mine kissing my knuckles. "I have never been so happy, baby. You make me feel so protected, so treasured, so loved... You ask me about my days, you care about my problems. You're my escape, from everything dark and sad and crazy. You've always been that. The best mistake of my life was dropping that list."

"I'm glad I found it." I captured her mouth in a deep kiss. "I'll happily spend the rest of my life making all your wishes come true."

Her mouth curved into a smile. "They're going to be mad at us, though."

I shrugged. "I don't give a fuck what anyone thinks. Except Des."

"That's why she knows." She wrapped her arms around me, hugging me tightly. "I just want to live in this little bubble we created a little while longer. Then, we can announce to the world that I'm your wife."

I proposed while she was showing me a new property. She fell in love with the house during the walkthrough. I told her to put in a bid, perched her up on a countertop, and asked her to marry me. Once we were settled in our new home, we started the wedding planning process but quickly realized the whole in-front-of-everyone thing didn't work for us. We eloped last month, with Des' blessing. Flew to Denver, rented an Airbnb, hired a photographer, and recited our vows to each other in a quiet, self-solemnization ceremony. No witnesses, no officiant. Just us.

"Best day of my life." I kissed her brow, resting my forehead against hers. "Hands down."

"Love you, Spence. So much."

I traced the line of her nose with my finger and placed a soft kiss to her mouth. "I love you too."

Alaiya had walked into my life in a Wonder Woman costume and changed my outlook on life, made me want to be a better man. I didn't know it then, but she stole my heart that day. The connection we formed had never waned, never buckled under the pressures of life. Then, one day ...

She dropped her list.

I fell in love.

And I planned to spend the rest of my life making her happy.

———

Subscribe to my Newsletter
New Releases, Upcoming projects, and Freebies!

# Four20 Bae Anthology

Smoke in Love by Elle Wright

Smoke N' Stroke by Aja

Smoke Before the Release by Kelsey Green

Smoke After Hours by Sherelle Green

Taste the Smoke by Sheryl Lister

Smoke Screen by Kimmie Ferrell

Touch of Smoke by A.C. Arthur

Smoke & Mirrors by Angela Seals

Embers and Smoke by Tiye

I fake laugh every time I think about how ironic it is to be a commitment-phobe relationship therapist who is also the daughter of two world-renowned marriage and family counselors. Seriously, it's comical!

Want to know how I messed up my life? Getting arrested for stealing a priceless artifact for a tearful client.

Want to know what my biggest problem is? Spending my life teaching women how to break relationships when all I want to do is make a relationship—with him.

Want to know what that makes me? The Break-Up Expert who is questioning everything I thought I knew.

# Excerpt: It's Not Me, It's You

## YOUNG IN LOVE, BOOK ONE

"**W**ell?" A soft smack to my ass followed the question, pulling me from a peaceful slumber.

I couldn't open my eyes, though. I couldn't even stretch like I normally did when I woke from a much-needed nap. If I did either or both of those things, I'd give myself away. Because there was a man behind me, a penis inside me. And I'd actually fallen asleep—during sex. *There's a first for everything.*

Things had seemed promising tonight. Tasty food, sensual music, stimulating conversation. Dr. Donell Pointer had hit all my superficial checkmarks for consent. *Looks*. Sincere brown eyes, pretty white teeth, strong body. *Voice*. He sounded like hot sex on a smooth, dark chocolate stick. *Personality*. The good doctor had charisma. I'd laughed at his jokes and had even enjoyed a debate on why soulmates didn't exist. Of course, he'd landed on the they-do side of the fence, while I'd stayed firmly on the no-the-hell-they-don't side. I wasn't one of those women... I didn't believe in soulmates or that love-at-first-sight bullshit. The only way to fully love someone was if you *knew* them. Fight me. But even though he was a sappy son of a bitch, it was okay. Because he'd earned a check in my most important wet-panties category. *Smile*. Oh. My. God. That thing lit up the room. And the tiny creases around his full lips made my decision easy. Sex. All night, preferably. But at least two times.

Except, I couldn't get through *one* time without a smidge of drool on the pillow, and not because he'd knocked me out with his prowess. Dr. Donnell was definitely fine as hell. Too bad he had no fuck game. No back-breaking. No tongue-talking. No toe-curling orgasm. If brown liquor was the devil, there had to be a worse name for bad, boring, small-ass dick. Hell? Disappointment? Underwhelming? No, tragic? Yep, that's it.

"Blake?" His low voice broke my reverie.

Sighing, I opened my eyes slowly. *Damn*. Such a shame to be so hot, yet so limp. A nod and a forced smile later, I rolled over on my back and tried not to look at his *little* problem. "Where is my...?" I spotted my dress on the floor near the door. Before I could slide off the bed and race toward the bathroom, his hand wrapped around my wrist.

"Baby, where do you think you're going? I'm not done with you."

*Oh, boy*. I couldn't help the hard roll of my eyes. *Lord, I promise to do better and not be a hoe if you'll just get me out of here without me having to hurt this man's feelings*. He was a friend of a friend of an associate. The last thing I needed was friend-group gossip. "I have to leave. Early meeting." I offered him another smile and a light caress on his cheek.

He pulled me closer and nuzzled his nose against my neck. "How about you stay? We can have breakfast in the morning. Together."

Shit. He just said the magic, dirty word. *Together* was not what's up. "No need. I really have to go." I slipped out of his arms. But that hand of his remained on my wrist.

"I want to see you again. Maybe you'll give me a chance to change your mind about soulmates."

*Like hell.* "Not likely," I grumbled. "So, about that." I scratched my head, scrambled to find the right words. Somehow, "fuck off" seemed too harsh. "We don't have to do this. If you haven't realized yet, I'm not one of those women who needs the obligatory 'let's get together soon' speech." Shrugging, I continued, "It's probably best if we just not even try."

"Blake, you're a beautiful woman."

*Can he just shut the hell up?*

"I had a good time with you tonight." He brushed his thumb over my nipple.

*I really have to find my panties.*

Donnell rubbed his nose over my cheek and placed a chaste kiss there. "I don't want this to end."

*Okay, I can live without my panties.*

A mix between a groan and a whimper escaped his lips as he cupped my pussy in his palm—his *small* palm.

*How the hell didn't I notice this?*

"You're so beautiful," he whispered against my ear. "I want you."

*Fuck the panties and the bra.* I gripped his hand before his finger made contact with my clit. "Okay, stop. I'm done here." I pushed him away, stood, and picked up my dress.

"Blake?"

I rolled my eyes, slipping my dress on quickly. Luckily I'd chosen the comfortable, flowy maxi dress over the sexy, short black dress I'd considered wearing. Turning to him, I met his waiting, pitiful gaze. "Dr. Pointer, thanks for tonight. But I'm not interested in more of this." I motioned toward the bed. "It was…" I stopped short of saying it was nice, because I made it a habit not to lie. "Thanks for dinner and the… conversation."

Bolting from the room, I slammed the door shut and leaned against it to catch my breath. I ran my fingers through my probably fucked-up hair and hurried out of the hotel.

**TAYLAR**

I'm a professional. I have strict rules of conduct when it comes to my business, Taylar Made Events.

My number one rule? Don't flirt with the groom.

But... What about the groom's moody, but *hot* brother?

**KEON**

When I agreed to pay for my brother's wedding, I didn't know he was marrying the Wicked Witch of the East. I also didn't realize I'd find myself fantasizing about the wedding planner.

The Problem? She's my best friend's little sister. The curve of her hips and the fullness of her lips are none of my business.

Now... I just have to remember that.

# Excerpt: Some Kind of Love

## A SMOKE AND BURN PRELUDE

"Fuck you and that bitch you brought home last night!"

It's not that hard. Really. *And I'm smart, dammit.* Except when I confused *good* dick with *good* guy. Somehow, I'd failed that test time and again. At this point in my life, I should've learned my lesson. I didn't consider myself a true playa, and trust me... I knew several women who got theirs and kept it moving. More power to them. That just wasn't me. Aside from a single one-night stand in college, I preferred sex within the safe confines of a monogamous relationship. Yet, I couldn't even count the number of times I'd been betrayed by a beautiful dark chocolate dick attached to a fine-as-hell weird-ass, stupid-ass, jealous-ass muthafucka with baggage. This time, though, I was caught up in a love spat between my "man" and the woman who had a key to his house and called herself his girlfriend.

The woman banged on the bedroom door. "Come out, Bitch!"

*This can't be my life.* My family had always teased me about my taste in men. My father called me a bum magnet. Based on my last several boyfriends, my dad might've been on to something. I blamed him, though. It was his impossible standards that made me want to rebel. From the blind dates with his colleagues to the constant complaining about my singlehood, it was no wonder I was attracted to men who were the total opposite of what I knew my parents wanted for me. But Hector was different… or so I'd thought.

When we'd met at a fundraiser, Hector had impressed me. Mostly because he could speak to anything. Politics, sports, books, movies, food… He was an entrepreneur, a business owner who'd turned one real estate investment into several vacation rentals. During dinner last night, he reiterated his commitment to making me happy, to showing me he was serious about me. Which was why I'd gone against my own rules and went to his place. *Damn*. I couldn't believe the turn of events.

"Can you chill out, Chandra?" Hector grumbled. After ten minutes of her screaming at the top of her lungs about betrayal, broken engagements, and countless lies, this nigga finally spoke up. "What the hell are you doing here? I'm single."

Another loud knock or five later, Chandra shouted, "When I see her, I'm fucking her up!"

*My head hurts*. I considered climbing out of the window, until I glanced at my reflection in the mirror. The batshit crazy girl still spewing threats was right. All my shit was in the living room. With them. My lack of clothing and hangover was no match for her level of rage.

In my haste to get fucked, I'd left my keys, my dress, my purse, my shoes, and my common sense out there. I didn't even want to think about the lecture my mother would give me if she could see me now. Top of the list of things *not* to do is leave your purse in another room while you're sleeping. The sex had been amazing, though, starting from the moment he took me against his front door and ending with his tongue on my clit early this morning. *Damn*, my underwear was out there too? And my bra. And my phone. *Shit, Taylar, you fucked up.*

The only thing I had with me was my… I hurried to the bedside table and picked up my Apple Watch. Luckily, the battery hadn't died. I whispered a text to my brother who had my location: *Come get me. Now.*

A loud scream and the sound of broken glass on the other side of the door forced me to look for a weapon to protect myself, because… Shit, I had no idea what I'd find when I left the room. I searched his drawers, looking for something other than his t-shirt to wear. I found an oversized shirt and a pair of sweatpants, and quickly slipped them on. Climbing on top of the dresser, I flung open the blinds and bit out a low curse when I noticed the bars on the window.

The argument outside the bedroom was in full swing. As both of them hurled insults at each other, I practiced a karate kick and a weak-ass uppercut to the air. Only to fall back on the bed. Staring at the ceiling, I whispered to whoever I thought could hear me beyond the physical realm, "Granny, you once told me never to trust someone with shifty eyes, and I didn't listen. But he's so fine. And you told me to never drink that nasty-ass gin, but it's part of the Long Island so I did. It was good, though. Okay, God, I would tell you that I wouldn't have premarital sex, but you already know I'm a work in progress. I learned my lesson, though. Maybe. Please let me get out of this without having to fight. 'Cause y'all know I haven't lifted a fist since Hailey Palmer pulled my ponytail out during homeroom class in ninth grade. I'm not cut out for this. Amen. Oh, and—"

"Chandra, stop!" Hector roared, after the dog whimpered.

*Did she kick the dog?* I picked up the nearest weapon.

"That's my dog too," Chandra blared over the puppy's piercing bark. "I'm taking him with me!"

*What the hell are they doing out there?* I checked my watch. Ryker hadn't responded yet, but that didn't mean he didn't see the text. If anything, my big brother was already on his way to save the day.

The doorbell chimed, and I sent up a silent prayer of thanks. But the voice that pierced the silence wasn't Ryker. Wait a minute... "It's the police," I murmured to myself. My shoulders sagged as relief washed over me. Not only did I not have to fight, but I didn't have to use my handy dandy weapon either. I set the lamp down and tiptoed toward the door.

I listened as the cop assessed the situation, and then I took a chance and cracked the door open. All eyes landed on me, and I waved. "Hi."

I scanned the living room. Pillows were strewn on the floor, the dog was eating food that had spattered on the rug. Glass was shattered on the furniture and one of the officers was handcuffing the woman who continued to spew threats at me as I emerged from the bedroom.

I met Hector's gaze with a hard glare and fought the urge to slap the shit out of him for putting me in that situation. "Where's my stuff?"

"I ripped that shit up," Chandra taunted.

"Shut the hell up, Chandra," Hector growled. He handed me what was left of my dress. "I'm sorry. Can you stay? I'll make breakfast."

I raised a questioning brow. "You can't be serious."

Hector approached me tentatively. "I am. It's complicated."

"Obviously."

"Is that your Lexus SUV outside, miss?" an officer asked.

I nodded. "Yes. What's wrong?"

"Ms. Payne admitted to vandalizing the vehicle," he explained. "I'm happy to call a tow company for you."

"I can't drive it?"

The officer flashed a sad smile. "Not at this time. Not with four flat tires."

I murmured a curse. "Thanks, Officer. I'll take care of it."

Officer Kennedy led me over to the kitchen. After he took my statement, he gave me his card. "Thanks, Miss Cross. Can I drop you anywhere?"

I gathered the rest of my things. "That would be great."

A soft knock echoed in the quiet house. "What's up?" Hector asked, a hard edge to his voice.

"I'm here for her."

I recognized the voice immediately, and it wasn't my brother Ryker. It wasn't my other brother, Maddox either. I blinked. "Keon?"

Intense, dark eyes bore into me, raked over me, almost like he was checking every inch of my body to be sure I was okay. "You good?"

"Ryker sent you?"

"Are you good, Taylar?" he repeated, never breaking eye contact with me.

I swallowed. Growing up, my brother's friends had always treated me like their little sister. They got on my nerves, scared away every boy in school, and raided my stash of junk food all the time, but they'd always protected me. Even now, I could count on them to step in when Ryker couldn't.

My fourteen-year-old self would have sworn Keon secretly wanted me to be his soulmate for life. It was the way he looked at me that always made me question everything I thought I knew. Of course, he'd never done or said anything inappropriate. He'd never been anything but a perfect gentleman, even though I'd imagined whispered declarations of secret love, stolen glances, and steamy makeout sessions behind my brother's back.

"Taylar?" Keon called again.

"I'm okay," I croaked. "I'm fine. Thanks for coming."

"Can we talk?" Hector asked. "I—"

I brushed past him. "I have nothing to say to you."

Hector reached out to grab me, but I maneuvered away from his grasp. "Taylar, listen."

"You heard what she said." Keon glared at Hector. "Lose her number. You don't want those problems."

As I neared Keon, I realized I felt lighter, like I could breathe again. I felt safe. "I'm ready."

Keon searched my eyes, took my hand, and led me out of the house. The car ride back home was eerily silent. No doubt, I was grateful that he came. But the embarrassment I felt had eclipsed the gratitude.

I swallowed past a lump in my throat. "Please don't tell anyone about this." Tears welled up in my eyes. "I don't want my dad to find out."

Election day was right around the corner. The last thing my father needed was a scandal to prevent him from winning his heavily-favored race to become a member of the Michigan House of Representatives. The campaign had worked hard to get him to this point, and I hated the thought of being the reason he wouldn't be able to succeed.

"You know that's not who I am, Taylar." Everyone else called me Tay or sis, but Keon had never used a nickname to refer to me.

"Not even Ryker?"

He smirked. "Not even Ryker," he agreed.

I sunk into the leather seat of his truck. "Thanks. And… don't mention it. I mean, this. Ever again."

"Your secret is safe with me."

*Acknowledgments*

God is so good!

To my family and my *framily*, I love you all! Thanks for your patience and your support.

To my lit sisters… You already know. This journey wouldn't be the same without you. Thank you!

To Nicole… You always come in clutch. Love you!

To Midnight… Thanks for saving the day. Again!

A special shout-out to the awesome readers , bloggers, and writers that I've met on this journey. Thanks for your support. I appreciate you!

*Connect with Elle!*

Subscribe to my Newsletter
New Releases, Upcoming projects, and Freebies!

On Facebook,
Join my cocktail lounge for exclusive updates, drink recipes,
and lots of fun!
bit.ly/EllesCocktailLounge

Visit my website: www.ellewright.com

Email me at info@ellewright.com

Thank you for reading Spencer and Alaiya's story! I love to
hear from my readers. If you enjoyed *Smoke in Love*, please
consider posting a review or sending an email. They really do
help. Don't forget to tell your friends!

*About the Author*

There was never a time when Elle Wright wasn't about to start a book, wasn't already deep in a book—or had just finished one. She grew up believing in the importance of reading, and became a lover of all things romance when her mother gave her her first romance novel. She lives in Michigan.

*Connect with Elle!*
www.ellewright.com
info@ellewright.com

facebook.com/ElleWrightAuthor
x.com/LWrightAuthor
instagram.com/lwrightauthor
amazon.com/Elle-Wright/e/B00VMEWB78
bookbub.com/profile/elle-wright

*Also by Elle Wright*

## CONTEMPORARY ROMANCE

*Edge of Scandal Series*

The Forbidden Man

His All Night

Her Kind of Man

All He Wants for Christmas

*Once Upon a Series*

Beyond Forever (Once Upon a Bridesmaid)

Beyond Ever After (Once Upon a Baby)

Finding Cooper (Once Upon a Funeral)

*Jacksons of Ann Arbor*

It's Always Been You

Wherever You Are

Because Of You

All For You

*Wellspring Series*

Touched By You

Enticed By You

Pleasured By You

*Pure Talent Series*

The Way You Tempt Me

The Way You Hold Me

The Way You Love Me

*Distinguished Gentlemen Series*
The Closing Bid

*Women of Park Manor*
Her Little Secret

*Carnivale Chronicles*
Irresistible Temptation

*New Year Bae-Solutions*
One More Drink

*Young In Love Series*
It's Not Me, It's You
It's Not Love, It's Business
It's Not the Hookup, It's the Chase
It's Not Them, It's Only Her
It's Not Forever, It's For Now

*Baes of Christmas*
Ten Christmas Shots

*Smoke and Burn Series*
Some Kind of Love

*Baes of Juneteenth*
Mr. Down for Whatever

## HISTORICAL ROMANCE

*DECADES: A Journey of African American Romance*

Made To Hold You (The 80s)

## SUSPENSE/THRILLER

Basement Level 5: Never Scared